A Wall Within

By
Barbara Harned Dorsett

PublishAmerica
Baltimore

© 2003 by Barbara Harned Dorsett.
All rights reserved. No part of this book may be reproduced in any form without written permission from the publishers, except by a reviewer who may quote brief passages in a review to be printed in a newspaper or magazine.

First printing

ISBN: 1-59286-306-X
PUBLISHED BY PUBLISHAMERICA BOOK PUBLISHERS
www.publishamerica.com
Baltimore

Printed in the United States of America

DEDICATION

*I dedicate this to all who suffered child abuse
and are still struggling to recover.*

*I thank them for giving me this voice to show that
painful memories are pervasive, affecting life's quality.*

ACKNOWLEDGMENTS

To Al, I thank him for 56 years of his love and making me follow my dreams.

I thank Faith Berlin for her knowledgeable guidance... Betty McElhatten for helping me with her wordmanship and eight years with two writing groups whose invaluable critiques taught me to tighten and grow in my writing but always with encouragement.

I also thank Doris King for her friend Mary Goodell, who gave me a wall.

PROLOGUE

"Lucille!" His mothers voice called from the bathroom. "Lucille! Time for your bath!"

The young boy held a little metal car in his hands. The doors opened and closed; the back where most cars held groceries or suitcases opened to show a little molded engine. He ran his fingers over the sloped top. If it was bigger he imagined he would slide down over the window and front bumper except he wouldn't want to scratch it, not if it was his car. He would have one some day. A Volkswagen, that's what his dad said it was. "Lucille!" The voice became more serious. Lucille slowly closed the doors and the 'trunk' while getting off the floor of his bedroom. He gently placed the car on the table next to his bed. Yes, he would have a car just like this one someday. Blue, it would be blue. His favorite color.

"Come child, I have the water just the right temperature." His mother smiled at him, not angry that he had delayed the daily bath. "You are now four and this is a very special day and you want to be very clean." She pulled his shirt over his head and then removed his shorts and underwear. His bare feet were still covered with dried mud and sand as he had played outside just after a heavy rain. He knew they would get a bath-brush scrubbing this time and he was sure he would hear about the dirt he had tracked into the house. A noise at the small window in the bathroom caught his attention as he stood naked. Rain, a light rain ran down the glass, almost like tears.

The water was just right and he reached for his toys that lined the top of the tub.

"No! We don't have time for play. I need to get you sweet and clean as your father is waiting for you. Lucille, this is the day when you learn what it means to be a man." She smiled at her son, then lowered him into the water, making sure he was completely wet. "You will please your father and that will please me." He watched his mother rub the bar of soap over the face cloth many times, making the mound of suds he liked and then taking hold of his arm she pulled him up to a seated position and starting with his hair and face, washed him all over, twice checking and washing his bottom very carefully, making sure he had wiped himself clean. "MOM." "HUSH," she said as she went in ever deeper. Have you had a bowel movement today?" "Yes, after lunch." Lucille answered as he tried to pull away, looking at his mother for answers but she just picked up one of his feet, clucking at the dirt. She just scrubbed it with a soft brush while Robin, then laughing, wiggled the foot free before she caught the second one.

"There, I think you are ready. Let's get you dressed." Lucille always loved being patted dry with the big bath towel but this time his mothers fingers in the towel went everywhere and he was glad when she was sure he was dry enough and he could put on his favorite blue pajamas.

"Now then, let's get you dressed." His mother took a pair of girls white panties with lace around the legs from the chair and held them for him to step into. "They aren't mine!" He complained. "They are girls and I won't wear them...I want my pajamas!"

"I told you this is a very special time and you will wear what I have for you, for your father. Now, no more complaining, we are late already!"

Tears came to his eyes but he did as he was told. First the panties, then a dress that had no sleeves, a slip he had heard his mother call it. Then, NO! A dress with tiny pink rosebuds all over it was pulled over his head and quickly buttoned in the back.

Lucille had always hated his name as he had been kidded by the older boys at school. It was a girl's name and now he looked like one. His hair was always kept long enough to touch his shoulders. He didn't mind that as some of the big boys there in Hawaii wore their hair long and he liked to look like them but...now his mother had brushed his slightly damp hair, then parted it on the side, instead of the middle as usual and worst of all, tied a pink ribbon on it. Robin squirmed in his mother's hands, not daring to cry or speak up. This was for his father and it would please his mother, but...all he wanted was to show his father how he looked and then pull it off, put on his pj's and be back to being a boy as he climbed into his bed holding his little blue Volkswagen.

Chapter 1

Wayne stood back looking at the body at his feet, unable to believe what he had just done. He bent to check her pulse, there was none. He sucked in his breath, hardly able to move. She was dead! "Oh, God, NO!" He hadn't meant to kill her, **"God, Nooo! NO!"** He screamed... but she **was** dead! Blood was slowly pouring from her temple; her eyes open, staring at him, her mouth open as if still screaming her abuse. He staggered back, his knees buckling, he slowly slid down the wall. Vomit rose in his throat but he swallowed hard. He couldn't have that mingle with the stream of blood. He felt cold, yet beads of perspiration were wetting his forehead. He couldn't breath, he couldn't think.

He'd killed Aunt Mary and he'd killed his life. He put his face in his hands and sobbed.

He'd killed Erin's favorite aunt; a person she loved dearly, someone who had replaced her other when she had died too young. Erin knew her aunt could be overbearing, controlling, but took it for love, protection. Aunt Mary never having children gave all of her maternal feelings to Erin. The two older brothers didn't exist in her life.

The one pain in Erin's life was Aunt Mary's dislike of Wayne. Her aunt never accepted any male friend Erin had introduced to her so she wasn't surprised when Wayne wasn't accepted as a possible serious relationship. When they announced their engagement there had been an explosive confrontation.

Erin was the only girl he had ever loved, the only one who had ever loved him. He hadn't planned to kill her aunt but she lay dead in front of him. Aunt Mary had possibly gotten her way through her death but he couldn't let this happen. He couldn't let her...he couldn't lose Erin. Sweat was burning his eyes and he wiped his hand over his face. He was a murderer! He'd killed and their wedding was in one week.

He pulled his long legs close to his body so they wouldn't touch the aunt. He felt sick and almost faint. It had all happened so fast...

Aunt Mary had called him to come to her house, about noon, as she needed a shelf built in her kitchen pantry. His hope had risen...she could be softening and finally accepting the marriage...it wasn't to be. He'd taken his tool box, skill saw and measuring tape from his truck. After measuring the pantry wall he was about to leave for Home Depot for the needed materials when he realized her invitation had been a ruse.

She just wanted to talk with him. She just wanted to try once more to convince him he wasn't right for Erin. He would ruin her life. At first she seemed in control and had just talked about how he wasn't as educated as Erin, didn't have the social graces, didn't run with her friends, the marriage wouldn't work! She had gone on...throwing at him how Erin was simply fascinated with someone rough and uneducated...so different from the other young men she dated. Erin wasn't really in love with him and he had to see that she was making a terrible mistake. He had to give her up!

Then her voice had risen until she was almost screaming. **"You're trash! You're just trash! You're not worthy to have my niece,"** she **shrieked,** her face inches from his. Then she **spit**! Her phlegm covered his face.

Wayne heard his mother, saw her face curled with rage but he had never hit her. But, he'd shoved Mary with all his strength and she'd smashed against the screen door. In terror, but still fighting verbally, she ran into her bedroom. "See...**I was right.**

You will destroy Erin!. She will never marry you...she will never have the slip for her wedding dress. I was going to press it but now I'm going to tear it to shreds, she will need her slip so that will stop her. **You'll never have her! She's mine!** She's **my girl...NOT YOURS!**" Wayne followed into the bedroom and grabbed her arm as she reached for the slip.

Mary turned on him with her fury. "**She's mine! Do you hear me? She's always been mine! She's my baby...my only daughter...She won't be married to a *trash* like you!**"

Wayne still had the hammer in his hand when he ran to save Erin's slip. As Mary grabbed it from the end of her bed his arm went up and the hammer came down with full force. Without a sound Mary had dropped to the floor. Blood slowly running onto the rug. "**NO!**" he yelled.

Wayne put his hands over his face and sobbed. He had ruined it all. Erin's life and his. When the tears no longer came he wiped his face with his sleeve and feeling weak and exhausted, as if in a fog, he pulled himself up from the floor, avoiding the puddle of blood walked to the kitchen, put the hammer on the counter, picked up the phone receiver and carefully dialed the familiar number.

"Hi." He swallowed hard. "Glad I caught you home."

"Darling...do I hear bad news in your voice? you sound tired."

"Yeah. I have to go on the road for a week. Our month's honeymoon is going to leave some of my customers short so I need to go before our wedding. It's now or shorten the honeymoon which neither of us would want." He wiped his face.

"I know, but you said, when we planned the honeymoon, you would be able to be home the week before the wedding and now...oh Wayne I'm so disappointed!

"Darling, when are you leaving? I can see you before you have to leave, can't I?"

"Erin I wish you could but I have mapped out my schedule and I really have to fly. I'm about to leave now." Wayne put his hand over his eyes as his body shuddered.

"I'm sorry I had to do this to you but you will have a busy week just packing for a month in Hawaii."

"I'm not taking that much and besides, we decided on a small wedding so we could have more time together before the wedding and honeymoon."

"I know, Babe, but I really don't have much control over my customers' needs. I've been getting calls so realized I have no choice. I'll call you every night. Erin, you know I'd rather have you in my arms than staying in out-of-the-way motels. I love you kid. If I leave now, I'll be back that much sooner. I 'll be back Friday night, just in time for the big day. Hey, just keep remembering our kisses last night and make them last the week."

Wayne laid his head on the counter and tried to sound disappointed but not terrified.

"Darling, they are still burning my lips." she tried to laugh. "But Wayne, it isn't fair! Our wedding week and you won't be here. Darn that company anyway!"

"Hey, it's what will support us. I can't take any chances of losing this job. I had a hard enough time finding it with all of the down-sizing. It wasn't my fault I lost that other job in the big personnel shuffle...I was just one of the guys who lost out. Now I'm just lucky they are giving me four weeks off. Most companies wouldn't, you know.

"Wayne, it's because you are a wonderful salesman and they are lucky to have you and they know that. I've always told you that!"

He tried to smile and covered a moan. "I'm glad you're partial but you can show me how much you love me in a week. It's just a week, Babe. I'm sorry, but I gotta go. I don't like hurting you like this but it's something I really have to do. Just think of me out on that lonely road thinking of you. Love you. Bye." He hung up quickly. He couldn't force himself to move for a few moments. He tried to visualize Erin and her disappointment but all he could see was Aunt Mary's body on the floor next to her bed, the blood still running, staining a large spot on the rug. The vomit came quickly as he leaned over the sink and emptied his stomach in long, projectile spasms. Then the tears came again, deep sobs that shook his whole being and took his breath.

As his body quieted Wayne took a paper towel and wiped his eyes and then his face. He turned on the faucet to clean the sink and stood watching as if his life were going down the drain. He glanced at the kitchen clock. It was getting so late. He had so much to do before leaving.

Wayne looked at the hammer but couldn't bring himself to pick it up. The blood had to be removed. He wrapped a paper towel around his hand and picked up the hammer. He ran it under the hot water faucet, poured dish soap over it, rubbing it hard with his fingers, and rinsed it again. The sink would need more cleaning but he wondered if he would always see blood on his hands. He would never get it from his conscience. The screen door couldn't be fixed and certainly not replaced. Not now. Her body had molded the screening when he slammed her against it. He would try to push it back into place before he left but would have to be careful to not be seen working on it. Erin darling, I'm sorry, I didn't mean to do this. Oh, dear God, I didn't want to hurt her. How will we explain Aunt Mary not being at the wedding? Oh, God, what have I done? Erin wouldn't have left him. She loved him. They would have had their wedding in spite of what Aunt Mary had said. He felt sick but forced himself to move. How could he have let this happen...how could he explain this...? What would he do with the body? He would have to hide her. Erin couldn't know what he had done. But where? Where could he hide a body in this house? He couldn't carry it outside in the early afternoon and by night he had to be on the road. He had to have an alibi. It had to be here...someplace in the house. Wayne walked around the few rooms in the Spanish bungalow. A closet, he knew about closets, but no; it would be quickly found. A wall...he had once heard of someone building a fake wall to make room for a long dresser...but where? He looked at all of the rooms...at their walls. In the spare bedroom there were two small windows on separate walls, a closet on the third and the door on the fourth. The window on the wall across from the foot of the double bed seemed to have a flowering vine across it...blocking out much of the sunlight. He pulled the shade down to the sill and then drew the short drapes closed. The room didn't seem much darker. The window wouldn't be missed by anyone not familiar with the house. Would Erin miss it?

He knew she had stayed here a few times but he would have to take the chance...it was his only choice. A wall would only need to be a foot or so out into the room and he didn't feel that space would be missed. A foot or so might do it. Once again he used the measuring tape and laid it the width of the wall and then the height. Two, four by eight sheets of knotty pine paneling, trimmed a little in the width, would work. This room must have been paneled years ago.

He didn't feel knotty pine was popular in the 90's but hoped to find some at one of he lumberyards in San Diego. He wrote down his measurements for the shelf and paneling on a pad of paper and then added a box of nails before turning to leave the house. He couldn't lock the door as he didn't have a key and he wasn't about to search Aunt Mary's things for one. He had to be lucky and hope no one would come to visit while he was gone. He couldn't believe Erin's aunt had many friends but there were always neighbors.

He had been here before with Erin so even if he was seen he wouldn't be considered a stranger. He quietly left, unlocking and closing the door and then the screen door with Mary's body imprint on it. A mocking bird sat on a fence post singing its many happy melodies. He had once wondered if they actually copied other birds' songs or just made up tunes. Now he just wondered how anything could be so happy when he felt such misery.

Home Depot. He would go there first for the shelving and the two by fours for the bracing, and nails. The Depot was large...full of people. He probably wouldn't be recognized or remembered by anyone there...especially with his small purchase, but it wouldn't matter. Erin knew he had been asked to build a shelf and she too had been pleased that her aunt had turned to him for help in her home. Funny she hadn't asked about the project or asked to speak to Aunt Mary. She had been surprised and disappointed with his decision to leave immediately for Sacramento so she wasn't thinking about a pantry shelf. She hadn't even asked where he was, probably thought he was in his apartment. Wayne stopped for a minute, standing in front of plumbing supplies. It was still early, she couldn't have thought he was finished with the shelf, back in his apartment and ready to leave. He had made the call too early. God, could he have made a drastic mistake?" Too late to think about it but he had to move fast with his other purchase...get the job done and get out of San Diego.

From Home Depot, Wayne drove north to Pine Tree Lumber in Escondido. He had been there only once before and had found you could find the unusual there so was taking a chance on them for the paneling. He'd been lucky. They'd had several panels to choose from and he'd picked two he thought would match the old walls in the small bedroom. He bought them quickly, trying not to be too talkative or friendly with the clerk; genial but nothing more. All of the lumber had been loaded in the back of his small truck and Wayne headed back to La Jolla. Once there he parked in the driveway as close to the back door as he could. The older neighborhood was still quiet when he let himself back into the kitchen. He had seen no one and breathed a little more easily.

The hammer sat on the counter, blood still on its head. Was blood really there or just in his mind? He ran the hot water again and drenched dish soap all over it. Scrubbing this time with a stiff brush he found under the sink. The running water flushed off the rest of the drying blood but Wayne wondered if it wouldn't come back, if it wouldn't always return. He would build the shelf and the wall and then wash the hammer again to be sure it was clean before he packed it back in his toolbox. He'd have to be careful not to leave any evidence of what he had done. Wayne moved and thought almost as in a trance. The last two hours seemed almost unbelievable but they couldn't be erased. He couldn't undo the fact that he had murdered Mary Picard.

Wayne forced himself to hold the hammer and go to the kitchen pantry. He moved some of the bags of potato chips and a ten-pound bag of potatoes to one side of the little room and picked up the shelf wood. Aunt Mary had asked for a storage shelf at the bottom of the closet. He would put it up for her...the bitch! The dead bitch! The shelf was responsible for his being here. It was responsible for Erin's Aunt Mary being dead. He wasn't a violent person, he wasn't a murderer but now...Oh God, he **was**!

Wayne looked at the pantry. A closet. He hadn't realized how hard it would be for him to be working in that small area. He felt that somehow the aunt knew his problem with closets and had done this on purpose. Beads of sweat began to build on his face as he fit the shelf against the wall. Still on his knees, he backed out into the kitchen. Air...he needed more air. He stood and walked across the kitchen to the open door. He took deep gulps and felt better so he returned to the closet. Flashbacks! He'd tried so hard to forget his past and this damn closet was bringing it all back. Well, it wouldn't beat him. He would finish this shelf, as it would help to assure his future happiness. He had never been more determined and with his sleeve he again wiped sweat from his face. His eyes were burning from the salt and he felt his lungs were starving for oxygen but he kept hammering nails into the wood strips that would hold the shelf. He measured the wall length again. The sawing had to be done in the kitchen so he gratefully backed out of the closet and for a second time went to the back door for air. "Damn you! Damn you, Aunt Mary!"

Wayne quickly sawed the shelf to length and once again faced the confining room. He carefully maneuvered the board back into the pantry trying to avoid the full shelves above him. Cans of fruit, vegetables and soups. Boxes of cake mixes, biscuit mix, flour and sugar. He tapped the board into place and breathing a sigh of relief, backed out and found the broom to sweep up the sawdust. Leaning into the pantry he placed the bags of chips and the potatoes on the new shelf. It was better than she deserved.

The materials for the shelf had been removed from his truck

in the late afternoon when the neighbors could see him. He had casually dropped the Home Depot receipt on the kitchen floor. He had to think. Had to anticipate what Erin or the police would find.

He quietly returned to the truck and pulled the two panels from the floor and set both on the gravel, leaning them against the truck bed. He opened the screen door with difficulty; its bowed shape now made it ill fitting in the opening. One at a time, he carried the panels into the back bedroom. Then he returned to the truck for the framing wood.

He had stuffed the receipt from Pine Tree Lumber Yard in his pants pocket; proof of when he had purchased the paneling. Proof he had built the wall so he would destroy the receipt later. He carried the last of the lumber to the small bedroom. The mocking bird was now quiet.

Wayne looked around the room. A single bed with an old spread, a rattan bedside table, a round stained glass lamp hung above it and a rattan straight backed chair sat in the corner. Two small framed prints that looked as if they had been cut from a magazine hung on either side of the window, on the wall at the foot of the bed. Sparse and seldom used is what it said. A room eight feet by ten. No one would miss a foot from its length and that had to be enough. Both windows were hung with cheap, stained, dusty floral printed drapes. She could afford new drapes but she was cheap. Aunt Mary had accused him of marrying Erin for her money. He didn't want any of her money he just wanted Erin. He looked at the curtains again. He hated the small flower prints. His mother had always worn housedresses in small flower prints. Aunt Mary wore small flower prints and she reminded him of his mother in many ways, too many ways...God, too many ways!

He picked up his metal tape and measured out twelve inches

from the shorter wall. He then measured the width and height, laid his tape down and carefully removed the baseboards.

The framing of the short wall went quickly and he loosely set the panels against it. Slightly wide but that could be corrected by cutting off the outside tongue and groove edges from the two panels. It would be a perfect fit but not very strong. He knew the paneling would give in if anyone put a heavy pressure against his wall because he didn't have supports in the center. The window sill stuck out about eight inches. That would have to be enough support. He would have to chance it; putting the chair against the wall might protect it. Better yet, he'd check out the rooms to see if there was a dresser or table that could be moved to this room. Who would know it wasn't Mary's doing instead of his? Now came the hard part. Caching her body!

Wayne grabbed the kitchen towel and returned to Mary's bedroom. Moving as quickly as he could he wrapped her head in the towel, trying to soak the blood from the carpet as he did it. The blood was drying, he should have done this before he left for the lumber but the thought of returning to this room had been too sickening. He was now careful to not get blood on his clothes. How would he explain that? He held the covered head in his hands for a few minutes. He kept hoping Aunt Mary would suddenly move, prove she wasn't dead, he knew it wouldn't happen. He would just have to hide her, cover his actions and get out of there. He felt sick and forced himself to take deep breaths...the head moved with him. He let out a cry; the head fell from his fingers as he jumped to his feet. "Oh, dear God," he gasped and gulping for air ran back to the kitchen.

He'd never forget the sound of her head hitting the floor. He'd thought seeing the blood pour from her temple was the worst terror but this... he buried his head in his hands and leaned over the sink as he fought for control. Time was passing too quickly and he had to get out of there; splashing cold water on his face and neck helped.

In the pantry he found a box of large, black trash bags. He pulled out two, put the box back on the shelf and closed the door, he hoped for the last time! Wayne went back to the body. Blood was soaking through the towel, possibly from being dropped. He carefully pulled one bag over the wrapped head and then the shoulders avoiding the new blood, and then stuffed the lower body into the second bag, pushing the skirt with the small flower print down until it was completely covered with black. Wayne wiped sweat from his eyes, sucked in his breath, picked up the body and carried it to the smaller room and laid the thin woman on her side, just under the draped window. He pushed it against the outside wall as far as he could, tucking in any loose plastic, making it fit within the twelve inches. He carried a panel to the left side of the wall and nailed it to the framing, then nailed the second panel, covering the black plastic bags. She was gone! He breathed a sigh of relief. No more trimming needed except replacing the baseboard and he counted himself very lucky. He'd had lots of luck that day. Realizing what he had thought, he laughed a humorless laugh.

The new wall looked as if it had always been there. He replaced small nails in the wall for the pictures, noting they went clear through the paneling so he had to hang the prints carefully. Wayne stood back, observing his work. He had tucked his mother away in a closet but she was alive. He had now tucked Aunt Mary behind a wall but she was dead. They were both right. He wasn't any good!

Wayne replaced his hammer and extra nails in his toolbox, carefully checking the hammer one more time to be sure all blood stains had been removed. This time it seemed to be clean. He looked around the small house for a table or chest of drawers for the small bedroom. The living room looked crowded with furniture and an old oak chest looked as if it could be removed from between a large overstuffed chair, an end table and the couch without being missed. He found it quite heavy but by pulling in his stomach and lifting with his legs he slowly carried it back to the bedroom. He didn't want to drag anything. He couldn't afford to have new scratches on the floor.

Mary's bedroom. There wasn't anything he could do with the blood next to the bed. A small area rug was almost under the bed so he pulled it out to cover the bloody pool and thought it looked as if it belonged there...The room had to look as if someone had possibly come in and attacked Mary here in the bedroom. Police would find the hidden blood, would Erin? Would Erin, if she came in, realize Mary had been hurt or would she think she had just left in a hurry? In a hurry to escape going to the wedding! Erin wouldn't see the blood as long as she didn't move the small rug. He pulled the carefully made bed apart so it looked as if Mary had been caught in bed, or better yet, just left suddenly. The woman was always impulsive. He roughly pulled the spread back then the blanket and sheet. He mussed the pillow to look as if her head had been on it. Then he checked the bathroom. All seemed normal. The dining room...he hadn't been in the dining room and except for the removal of the chest from the living room it looked the same as it had when Mary had let him in this morning...God! Had it been only this morning? He had to think.

If Aunt Mary had left suddenly during the week to avoid the wedding, some of her clothes, personal things and a suitcase would be missing. He went to her closet to see if she kept a suitcase there. Her perfume almost overwhelmed him and he felt sick again.

He couldn't go in the woman's walk-in closet. There would

just have to be a mystery about her being missing and the broken screen door.

Wayne stood and thought about more details he would have to cover. Food! If Mary was there for a few days after he left he had to be sure she had food. He walked back to the kitchen and opened the refrigerator door. Almost no food, certainly not enough for her for the week. He would have to go out again to buy some. He didn't like the idea of being seen by neighbors or by a local grocery store this late. If she'd had food and this is what was left when she disappeared...he checked the dates on the milk and finding chicken and a steak in the meat compartment he checked them. They all had a few days to go. So, if she was here until the middle of the week she could have eaten these foods, or she could have had something else and planned to eat these later in the week. That wouldn't work so he put the meat in the freezer as Mary might have done if she had wanted to have them after their expired date. That was better. Beads of sweat started to cover his face again. The vegetables in the crisper...there wasn't anything he could do about them. They looked fresh enough now but he knew would look pretty bad in a few days. The bread drawer had a new loaf of bread so he removed a few slices and stuffed them in his pocket with the Pine Tree Lumber receipt.

Wayne slowly walked through the house again. What had he forgotten? The slip! Erin's wedding slip. Aunt Mary had promised to press it and then deliver it to her before the wedding. It should look as if she had prepared to do this a day or so before the wedding. Wayne looked in closets, found the iron and ironing board and set them up in the kitchen. He returned to Mary's bedroom and found the slip mixed in with the bedspread. He let his fingers feel the soft material, visualizing it on Erin then carried it to the ironing board and laid it across as if waiting to be pressed. She wouldn't have her slip for her wedding dress but somehow there would be an answer. He prayed Erin wouldn't come here to see the aunt and to get the slip. No, it was to be brought to her! She would expect it on the wedding day and would wait. How much pain would she feel when Aunt Mary didn't appear as promised. His poor darling. His poor darling, Erin.

Wayne stood by the phone in the kitchen. If he removed the receiver from the cradle it would ring busy each time Erin tried to call here but how long would it be before she would check with the operator... and then the house. If he left it to ring, Erin would think she wasn't home so wouldn't check the house. He left the phone as it was. He tried to think of anything else he had missed The lights. What should he do about the lights? He went into the bedroom and turned on the bedside table lamp and turned on her small television to a twenty four hour cable channel then changed his mind and turned it to channel 8. He remembered she liked some of the night shows on 8. The only television she had in the house. A nine inch black and white.

He drew the shade on the lone window in the bedroom, looked around and left, not looking back, carrying his tool chest and saw with him. Wayne left the house slowly, checking out the neighbors before he went out the kitchen door. Seeing no one, he let the door lock behind him and then the smashed screen door closed.

He opened the truck door, climbed in and sat for a few minutes there in the darkening day. What had he forgotten? He would have to quickly return to his apartment to pick up his traveling clothes and briefcase. Then he would leave immediately for Sacramento to see a customer in the morning. It would mean driving all night, checking into a hotel for a shower, change clothes, having a quick breakfast and then try to make some sales, just as he had told Erin he needed to do. Auto part stores in his territory were usually good for a few sales. He could use the commission but most of all he needed to be seen early the next morning in Sacramento. He would drive his regular route, make some sales and then return in time to be in La Jolla by Friday night. Saturday he and Erin would be married. Her brothers Joel and Jerry would be there from San Francisco. Doris Kettering, Erin's best friend would be her only attendant. His best friend Paul Jorgens would be his. A small service at A Wedding Chapel was all that was needed and the money they would have spent on a large wedding would go a long way on their Hawaiian honeymoon. It was Erin's dream. Hawaii wasn't his but he wanted her to have her dream.

Chapter 2

Wayne had a good week. He'd called Erin every night and her soft voice had been consoling. He had never felt more loved and was overcome with his love for her. The love his parents had offered was a sick love and he hadn't known anything else until he first saw those beautiful blue eyes. He'd escaped his parents when he was sixteen because he knew then that life was supposed to offer more. His life had not been normal, as he had been led to believe and he was determined to find out what 'normal' was.

The one thing his father had given him was a love and knowledge of cars. Their small yard was always full of old cars, some to be repaired, some for their parts. He had worked with his father from the time he was six until twelve when his father left the family. By then he felt he could build a car from the ground up if necessary. Cars were his passion, before Erin, and it had always helped him find a job. First as mechanics and then as a salesman for auto parts. He loved the work. He missed the smell of the grease you got when working around cars, but he could sell anything and he liked clean slacks and shirts instead of greasy overalls. He was sure he knew more about cars than his boss and for the first time he felt pride in himself and now an adorable girl loved him.

Life could be good. His life with Erin was going to be good. They would have their life and would have children who knew they were loved and were born from a wonderful love. Every child deserved that!.

How different would it have been if he had not been in a San Diego auto shop checking out supplies and had looked up from his order forms into the bluest eyes he had ever seen, then the sweetest smile. She had mistaken him for a clerk and he hadn't corrected her for the first fifteen minutes. Her car had died on the street just a block from the store and she was feeling quite helpless. A maiden in distress and he played Sir Galahad. He helped her find the right battery, retrieved the old battery then after she'd made her purchase he'd carried the new battery to her car and installed it. He didn't mind the grease he had gotten on his hands and the front of his shirt. He had loved every minute of getting dirty as it meant he could help this adorable young woman. San Diego was his territory that week and he felt it was fate. He hadn't had much experience with girls and was surprised how relaxed and comfortable he felt with this one. Once she realized he wasn't a clerk, she felt obligated to him. Someone was grateful to him and it felt wonderful.

Wayne had given her one of his business cards and she had given him her phone number. He didn't have her home address but knew he would use the phone number soon. Now here they were both very much in love and their wedding was to be on Saturday.

"Babe, I'm home and can hardly wait to see you. Did you have a good week?" He felt tense each time he spoke with her... fearful of what he would hear.

"Oh, Wayne. You were right! I was so busy at work and with organizing everything for the wedding, I wouldn't have had much time for you. I missed you but the days went so quickly...and now here you are, home again. The dinner is tonight and the wedding tomorrow. It has all come so quickly but honey, I can hardly wait to see you!

The boys are here in town at the Wind and Sea. They flew in from San Francisco this afternoon and Paul has promised to be at Jake's by seven. Can you pick me up and then

Joel and Jerry?"

"Sure, I just need time to take a shower and change clothes. I've been traveling all day and I wouldn't be very presentable as I am now. Sports jacket, slacks, shirt and tie still the dress for the evening?" The murder had filled his mind all week except when he was making sales. He had considered driving off the road to end the pain but his passion for her and the future he and Erin could have kept him going. Now, back in La Jolla the horror of what he had done was eating away at his stomach. How could he face her?"Yes, you don't mind very much do you? Oh, Wayne, I can hardly wait!"

"Me too, and Erin, I'd wear a full suit of armor if you asked me to." He tried to sound humorous with only the wedding on his mind. "I'll be at your place by six thirty and then we can pick up your brothers." He swallowed hard and then said. " Oh, wouldn't you like us to pick up Aunt Mary too?"

Erin's voice became soft and concerned. "Darling, I haven't been able to reach Aunt Mary all week. I'm not going to worry as her schedules are usually pretty hectic, besides, she did promise to have my wedding slip at my place before I got dressed. Wayne, I know Aunt Mary didn't want us to get married but she wouldn't miss my wedding. She wouldn't do that to me...would she?" Wayne held his face in his hand.

"No, I can't believe she would. She wouldn't hurt you that way...no matter what she thinks of me. If she does, well we will just have to go on with our lives and let her live hers the way she wants to. Your aunt is very opinionated, you know that, and she doesn't forgive easily either. You are the only relative she has really accepted. Joel and Jerry don't exist for her as far as I have been able to determine. I think they have just written her off, from what you've said. Your aunt will be the loser if she breaks off her relationship with you because of me. Erin, I would feel terribly guilty if I caused you that pain, but darling, I would do everything I could to make your life happy, to fill any void she left in your life. You know how much I love you and we are going to have a wonderful time building our life together. I've found love and true happiness for the first time in my life and I hope you feel the same. We have been blessed with something wonderful and tomorrow our lives really start. Now, the sooner we get this evening going the sooner tomorrow will arrive." He laughed. "But right now you wouldn't believe how much I need a shower."

"Wayne, wait. I do love you. You know I do and yes, we have been blessed. .Thanks for what you said about Aunt Mary. Yes, we can build our own lives even if it has to be without her."

Wayne hung up the receiver, sucked in his breath and headed for the shower. He felt unbelievably dirty.

Chapter 3

Erin stood in the doorway to her apartment on Turquoise. Wayne sucked in his breath for the second time that night. She was wearing an ankle length dress with a rounded neck, short full sleeves and a small print of pale pink roses. He grabbed her and held her close. Erin wasn't his mother and she wasn't her Aunt Mary. She was Erin, the sweetest most loving, considerate person he had ever known in his life and she was about to be his bride. He covered her face with kisses. The evening would be beautiful and she would never know how ill her dress had made him feel.

Doris Kettering peeked around the corner of the door. "Hey you guys...come up for air." She laughed. "You'll have the entire month to do that."

Embarrassed, Wayne greeted Erin's best friend. "Doris, hi. Sorry I wasn't around to help you move out of here. I thought we were to pick you up at your apartment."

"Relax. You sound like a nervous groom. No! I'm still here but we are supposed to pick up Joel and Jerry on our way to the restaurant. It's going to be a tight squeeze in that back seat with the three of us but I'll try not to complain." she laughed again. A contagious, hearty laugh.

Wayne, keeping one arm around Erin, reached out to Doris who came forward to join the embrace of her friends.

Erin had been her best friend since high school and she'd known Wayne for the

past year. It had been wonderful watching the two of them fall in love although she always suspected that Wayne had fallen for Erin that first day. She knew it was one of those beautiful rare loves that comes to only a few.

Wayne never talked about his childhood or where he was from so she felt it hadn't been a happy life. She and Erin had discussed it but Erin was so in love with this fine man she didn't care about his past. She'd vowed to do everything she could to see that his future, with her, would be perfect by giving him the love he'd never had. They would have family and friends around them. Paul Jorgens, from the company Wayne had left the year before because of down-sizing, seemed to be Wayne's only close friend. This was hard to understand because Wayne was a fun, thoughtful guy and went out of his way to avoid hurting anyone's feelings. Doris was a little sorry she hadn't met him first but he'd had eyes only for Erin and she deserved the love he had for her.

The three pulled apart and dramatically, Doris stepped back to admire Wayne's appearance. It was the first time she had seen him with a jacket and tie and she had to admit he looked pretty handsome. Not many men of their generation were crazy about suits and ties so some companies were now more relaxed about office wear, especially here in San Diego. Women lived in casual suits or slacks with a blouse or jacket. Skirts were often short. This made it hard to keep your dignity but this was what was accepted. Unfortunately not all women have good looking legs. Her mother used to reminisce about her day when you wore a hat, gloves, stockings and heels with a smart suit to work. You showed respect for your place of business and your company. She was appalled at the present styles and didn't let you forget it until her death two years ago but had taught Doris how to dress her figure. Long skirts or slacks covered her full knees and shoulder pads filled out her narrow shoulders. She had accepted that not all women had perfect figures. Hers wasn't perfect but it could be worse.

For tonight they had decided on long skirts and she wore a

light weight, peacock blue silk skirt and jacket with a silver bead necklace, matching earrings, silver shoes and carried a small silver bag. Erin's rose print dress came to her ankles, just showing pale pink sandals. A narrow string of her mother's pearls lay below her throat. Dangling pearl earrings hung from her ears. Her softly curled blonde hair rested on her shoulders and framed her little pixie face. She looked as a bride should look the night before her wedding. Doris smiled at Wayne who seemed overwhelmed.

The drive to the restaurant couldn't start soon enough. Erin's brothers had been down to San Diego only once this last year and she was eager to see them again. She had seen them through the years as she and Erin were growing up. A schoolgirl crush on Joel had brought Doris nothing but schoolgirl pain. He never knew she was around except when the girls were making nuisances of themselves. That didn't stop Doris from dreaming about the tall, handsome athlete who seemed able to be tops in everything he did. Jerry, eight years older was out of high school by the time the girls entered. He had gone on to college at UCLA and lived on campus so was home only for family special occasions and a few weekends when he longed for home cooked meals. Then Doris was busy with her own family's celebrations so she didn't see the brothers. She felt excitement build ...seeing Joel again...oh gosh, what would he think of her now?

"Paul will probably be early at the restaurant, so it's time to leave. The boys will be on the street waiting for us." Erin said. Her own excitement showing.

Doris suddenly remembered the missing Aunt Mary. "Erin, have you heard anything from your aunt yet?"

Erin's face sobered. "No, not a thing but Wayne has reminded me that if she doesn't show it's her loss...only it's mine too. I have always loved her so much." Her face brightened. "Come on, let's leave. I'm getting hungry and I can hardly wait to be with Joel and Jerry." She suddenly turned to Wayne. "Darling, it will be better if Aunt Mary doesn't come. She hasn't spoken to the boys for years and that could make it a very uncomfortable time for them. Maybe when she heard they would be coming she decided to leave town. I don't know why I didn't think of that before now."

"Erin, I think you hit it." God, wrong word. " I think that's just what she did so let's forget about her for now and have a great evening with friends and family who love you." He gave her a quick kiss and let out a silent breath. He tried to remember...Oh, God...the TV and bedroom light. He shouldn't have left them on. She wouldn't have left them on if she was leaving town. He swallowed hard. Had he blown it? A knot formed in the pit of his stomach as he turned to the young women and forced a smile. "You guys ready to leave?"

Doris felt her heart skip a beat when she saw the handsome blonde man standing with the good looking but shorter, brunette man. My God, Doris thought. I haven't gotten over the crush yet. This is going to be an interesting evening if I can get up the nerve to even speak to him.

The 'boys' piled into the car, one from each side to allow Doris to sit in the middle of the back seat. One at a time they leaned forward to give their little sister a kiss and patted Wayne on the shoulder.

"Are you all right, Doris? You aren't too squeezed?" Erin asked.

Are they kidding? Doris thought as she felt the strong tight thighs against hers. "No, thanks, I'm fine. Besides, the ride won't be long enough...I mean it won't be a long one." She flushed and the others broke into laughter.

Lord, why do you often say what you are thinking and not what you mean to say?

Now she had made a real fool of herself and the evening was still young. Doris remained silent the rest of the ride but the others filled the air with questions about Wayne's week, the flight from San Francisco and the plans they had for their return flight almost immediately after the reception.

Erin had been terribly disappointed when she heard their schedule but felt grateful to them for making the trip for the wedding. They were her only family left except for Aunt Mary and it would have been hard on her to have just Doris and Paul with her on this fabulous occasion. Her first and only wedding and it had to be a day she would never forget.

Paul was standing in front of the restaurant and quickly opened a back door and helped Joel out of the packed seat. Joel turned back to offer Doris his hand and then his arm to escort her into the restaurant. Doris gave him a self-conscious smile but could say nothing.

Wayne had gone around to help Erin. Jerry piled out by himself, shut all of the doors then slipped into the drivers seat to take the car to the lot. The wedding party entered Jake's to confirm their reservation at this distinguished restaurant by the sea. A popular place with the La Jolla residents as well as tourists. When the surf was high reservations were almost impossible to get. It was exciting to watch the waves pound the beach and rocks. They seemed to reach up to the diners.

Their table was in front of a large plate glass window. A glorious red sunset filled the sky and the almost full restaurant was quiet as the diners each had their own thoughts while watching nature's beauty. Wayne almost froze. Blood red! Would he never escape the vision of Aunt Mary lying in her own blood? He seated Erin then sat with his back to the sun as it dipped below the horizon and the sky darkened.

As the sun set, the candles on the tables began to give a warm glow to the room. Wayne wasn't sure how he would get through this evening. The knot became tighter.

Jerry was at the table almost immediately after they were seated. He leaned over Erin and gave her a sound kiss. "The greeting in the car wasn't adequate, sis." Not to be outdone Joel pushed back from his seat and gathered the petite blonde sitting next to him in his arms and gave an even longer kiss. Erin began laughing so hard she would have fallen from her chair if Joel hadn't held her even tighter.

"You two. I adore both of you and thanks for that welcome but we are in a public place." She laughed again.

"How about a drink so we can have a toast for the bride and groom?"

"A great idea but who is going to be the designated driver? I hate to spoil someone's evening but rules are rules." Jerry said as he pretended great seriousness.

"I." Paul said with great dignity. "I shall be the designated driver except that we have one problem." He laughed. "I drove my own car...I didn't come with you."

"Oh, damn," Jerry said with a scowl, still pretending great concern. "There must be some way to work this out."

Doris held up her glass of water with great ceremony. "I shall drive this family home safely after I have had a fabulous dinner. I and I alone." She took a sip.

Joel looked at Doris with admiration. "Doris, you've saved the day. How can we ever thank you?"

Doris, feeling slightly intoxicated from Joel's attention said. "I'm sure you can find a way."

The group laughed and gave Doris a quiet cheer as many in

the restaurant were now watching the party. Erin was uncomfortable with scenes so was waving her adored men folk down. If they were like this now, how would they be after they'd had a few drinks and she began to be fearful of a toast to the bride and groom. They should have asked for a more private room.

Wayne put his arm around her shoulder but didn't give her a kiss, knowing she was already embarrassed by her brothers' exuberance. That kiss and several others would come later this evening and even more tomorrow. Tomorrow...would tomorrow ever come? Would they really be allowed the happiness they had looked forward to? Why had he had two women try to ruin his life?

Chapter 4

Erin and Doris had a last 'sleep over' party. They hadn't had much need for food after the lavish restaurant dinner but ice cream sundaes, while sharing Erin's queen size bed, had seemed just right. How many times had they done this as children? During their teen years when the conversations had been about boys and Doris had confessed her crush on Joel. Tonight after driving the 'boys' to their hotel they had each given her a little kiss before kissing Erin goodnight. The feel of Joel's kiss was still on her lips. She was sure the chill of the ice cream wouldn't wipe it away. Wayne and Erin had about half an hour alone in the living room while Doris was discreet, staying in the single bedroom watching television.

Both girls had been so excited they were sure sleep would never come but they wakened to brilliant sunshine, their empty ice cream bowls still next to them. The spoons had spread chocolate on the quilted bedspread.

"This is it Doris! This is my wedding day. It's finally here." Erin looked at her friend lying so close to her. "Oh, Dor. I hope you will find your big love soon. I want you to have the same happiness I have." She took Doris' hand and held it for a few minutes. "Do you realize this is our last 'sleep in,' after so many we have had through the years. We have reached a milestone, I guess. We are finally adults and I'm going to miss all of the wonderful past years. It's kind of sad."

Doris rolled to her side and pulling her hand from Erin's, put her arm around her friend and held her close. They lay together for a few minutes, each feeling a closure in their lives. They were twenty-one now and their lives would be going in different directions. They would always be close friends...that could never change, but with Erin married it couldn't help but be different. Wayne's few things would be moved into this apartment where she and Erin had spent so many fun hours. Erin had cleaned her clothes closets, making room for his things. The furnishings were from her parent's home. She and the boys had chosen what they wanted when their mother died from breast cancer. Erin had spent hours in her mothers home with her mother; nursing, loving, supporting as much as she could until she died in her own home, in her own bed, there in La Jolla. The 'boys' had flown down frequently during her illness. They had always been a close family but with the second parent gone it was the closing of probably the biggest chapter in their lives. Fred Adams had passed on from prostate cancer four years before his adored wife. That had been the family's first blow. Lydia Adams hadn't met Wayne but the two girls knew she would have supported his growing relationship with Erin. She would have seen how much in love they were and felt he was a fine, stable young man.

Wayne had collected furniture and appliances from garage sales so had no attachment to them and would find it easy to give it all to a Thrift Shop. Wayne and Erin planned their move after the honeymoon.

Doris sat up in the bed while Erin lounged for 'just a few more minutes.' Doris smiled because she had a secret from her friend. She and Paul had planned together to get Wayne moved and his furniture donated while they were gone. Doris looked around this familiar bedroom. Except for adding Wayne's clothing and personal things this room would remain the same.

Wayne had some linens they could use. Doris knew he had never purchased anything except white. Sterile...and she wondered if this reflected something from his unknown background. The only fault Doris had noted, if you could call it a fault. Wayne was a cleanliness fanatic. He showered two to three times a day and changed his clothes each time. She wondered how he kept up with his laundry. How would Erin adjust to this? She was neat but dusting and laundry were not first on her list. They both knew the differences in their personalities and Erin felt they could work it out. Doris wondered if this could be the first real hurdle for this couple. Her precious Pisces friend, fun loving and artistic. She looked down at Erin. Her blonde hair, usually pulled back into a ponytail, was loose and lay on her pillow. Her beautiful blue eyes never looked so blue or so bright. She smiled up at her best friend.

"Well my dear girl. I guess this is it. We've had many chapters in our lives and it is hard to close this one but you will be opening a new, exciting book so we'd better get busy with breakfast. We need to be at the chapel in four hours." Erin threw back her covers and gave one bounce on the mattress and was standing looking at the floor. Two dessert bowls and two teaspoons had gone flying across the room. The spoons had hit the lone dresser and were now beneath its front legs. The bowls sat upright in the middle of the room. Startled, the young women burst into laughter.

"Oh my gosh. I forgot. Thank goodness we'd finished the ice cream but look at the chocolate on the sheets. Well, they needed to be changed today anyway."

Doris laughed. "Don't worry about them, Erin. This is your wedding day; you don't need to be changing sheets. I'll see they are washed along with the towels before you're home from your honeymoon."

Erin gave her friend a hug. "Thanks. I really didn't want to do it today. We really could remake the bed when we get home. You know, Wayne and I could make it together. That's romantic stuff but I guess we'll be making beds during our honeymoon so, except that it would be in our first home it would be better to have it done beforehand." Erin laughed. "I hadn't expected the sheets to be stained with bittersweet chocolate, but thanks, I really appreciate your doing that chore."

Doris began stripping the sheets. She could at least be this far ahead of the job and she didn't want the chocolate to set more then it already had. The slip. The wedding slip that Mary was suppose to iron and bring to Erin. Erin was in the shower so Doris slipped into the living room where her phone call wouldn't be overheard.

The phone rang and rang and after eight rings Doris gave up. Mary obviously wasn't home and probably would not be at the wedding of her so-called favorite niece. Doris cussed. Erin's dress was lace and needed a long slip and there wasn't time to shop for another. Long slips were not easy to find except in the department stores down in the valley.

The solution came as a flash. Her slip was white and would fit Erin. Her pale blue chiffon dress was lined and didn't really need a long slip. She could wear a half-slip that came below her knees. She went to the closet and took out Erin's wedding dress. White Belgium lace with a scoop neckline and short sleeves. It hung straight from the underarms, just touching Erin's hips. She'd wear white stockings and sandals and her mother's pearls. A short veil fastened to a Juliet cap would cover her long curled blonde hair. A bride's dress for any chapel and perfect for a morning wedding.

Doris hung the padded bridal hanger on the ceramic hook at the back of the bedroom door. Then, taking her dress from the closet she removed the long white slip that hung over the same hanger and transferred it to the wedding hanger. She found a half slip in Erin's lingerie drawer and held it at her waist. It went just below her knees. Perfect, so she placed it with her dress and felt both pride and a deep sense of relief. Aunt Mary Picard wasn't needed after all.

Erin walked out of the bathroom tossing her hair in a blue towel. Her body still glistened with water and Doris felt a pang of jealously. This tiny body was so perfectly constructed even though slim as a young boy. Stripped of any makeup and with her hair tossing around her face she looked like a fifteen-year-old instead of twenty-one. Erin didn't enjoy being compared with a teenager. At this time of your life you want to be older, not younger. Employers hadn't taken her seriously until she found a young dentist who hired her and her sweet personality as his receptionist. She'd taken some medical bookkeeping courses and computer training and his practice had grown, especially with admiring young men and elderly patients. The dentist had found a jewel and was concerned when he heard of her approaching wedding. He knew the groom was out of town frequently as a salesman and was relieved when she assured him she wanted to stay with her job.

"Doris! My slip came. Aunt Mary was here? She didn't wait? She didn't want to see me?"

Doris looked at her friend who stood holding her towel and looking at the wedding dress and slip on the back of the door. Her face was shining with happiness but her eyes were questioning.

"Nooooo, Erin." Doris said softly. I didn't think we should wait so that is my slip.

I realized I didn't need it so I borrowed one of your half-slips. You don't mind?"

The little face clouded over but then she smiled. "You're always coming to my rescue, all these years you have rescued me from tight situations. You were with me during the months my parents were ill. Now you're with me, supporting me again, rescuing me from my problem on my wedding day. How will I ever get along without you? Erin held her friend close. "Wayne loves me but I don't think he would have come up with this solution." She smiled and tightened her arms. "Thanks, Dor.," she whispered into her neck. You've done it again but are you sure you don't need the longer slip?"

Doris laughed to lighten the mood. "Not as much as you do. I think you in that lace dress without a slip over your beautiful slim figure would break up your wedding. You would drive all of the men mad, mad, mad." She gave Erin a strong hug.

"Oh poo, but the concept is pretty funny...I would have had a problem... thanks again but I hoped... when I saw the slip, I couldn't understand why she wouldn't have wanted to see me." Doris pulled back and looked at her friend. She heard the pain in her voice and could see the pain in her eyes and was going to comfort her when Erin changed the subject. "But, now it's your turn in the shower. I'll curl my hair while you wash and then you can use the iron. Oh, Doris, I am happy. All is so right with my world. despite my disappointment." Grinning, Erin gave her friend a hug and then pushed her to the bathroom.

Paul picked the girls up at eleven to allow plenty of time to get to the chapel. He wore a dark navy suit with a white shirt and a light blue tie. He was taken aback when he saw the two young women standing in the apartment door waiting for him. He had always thought they were cute but today they were both beautiful and Erin was the most beautiful bride he had ever seen. He could hardly wait to see Wayne's face when he saw her and why hadn't he really seen Doris before? He vowed to change that right away, then he remembered he would be working with Doris when they moved Wayne's things to this apartment. He decided to stretch that day as long as he could.

When Paul drove up in front of the wedding chapel Joel and Jerry were waiting at the curb and escorted the girls from the car. Joel had quickly presented his arm to Doris and it hadn't gone unnoticed by Paul. He was grateful the brothers lived hundreds of miles away as it would give him the advantage and he smiled as he drove to pick up the groom.

Jerry carefully kissed his kid sister and told her how beautiful she was. He took her arm and held it close to his side as he helped her up the steps to the chapel door.

The chapel looked like an old steepled church right out of new England. When they went through the doors they were surprised how small it really was. The dark brown pews, about ten rows, were divided by a single aisle. An aisle so narrow Erin realized two people could barely walk together. Certainly not three. Erin had wanted Joel and Jerry to both 'give her away.' How could she possibly choose between her precious brothers? They were her family. Paul was Wayne's friend and would be the best man with Doris her maid of honor, but what could they do about Joel and Jerry?

Erin sat in the last pew looking at the aisle, wondering how many brides had walked past these ten rows, wondered how they handled the narrow aisle, then she smiled. She had the solution. Paul would enter first with Wayne. Joel would walk down the aisle with Doris. Yes, she had noticed the attention they had paid to each other. Jerry would escort her behind Joel and Doris. Then, Doris would stand in front of the minister with her, Wayne and Paul. Joel and Jerry would sit in the first pew on the bride's side. That would work except Wayne would have no family on the groom's side. He didn't seem concerned but it hurt her. She had often asked about his family, about his past but he claimed to have no family and an uninteresting past and then he'd change the subject. but...he had to have family somewhere...someone who cared. Friends? Why wouldn't he want them with him on this special day? How sad they couldn't be here this morning. She sighed. Maybe she should have pressed him further before this...but now it was too late. No, she would ask Jerry to sit on the grooms side. It would balance the picture and they didn't need a bride side and a groom side. It was a small family wedding. She stood and joined Doris who immediately escorted her to the 'Brides' Room.'

A hand printed sign BRIDE was on the door next to the one marked 'Unisex.'

The Bride's Room had a dressing table for last minute hair and makeup repair, a clothes rack for brides who chose to dress there before the wedding, a small table and some straight backed chairs for 'waiting.' On the table were two flower boxes with the name Adams on them. Doris opened each and handed Erin a small white rose bouquet. She took out a second with pink and white roses for herself and then four boutonnieres; three in pink, one white. Doris opened the door and motioned to Joel to take the flowers for their lapels and to suggest to Jerry that he sit across the aisle to be in front of Wayne. The organist started the wedding march and the procession moved slowly down the aisle. Wayne turned to face them. He smiled and acknowledged Doris and then lifted his eyes to see Erin. Jerry almost laughed at the look on Wayne's face. First surprise and then the widest grin he had ever seen. Jerry glanced down at his sister and her look of adoration for her groom made him happy but envious for what she had and he hadn't yet found.

It was a short but beautiful wedding. Wayne's eyes had been so full of love as he repeated his vows and tears had filled Erin's. She had never been happier and hadn't felt this fulfilled or complete since her parents died. Her parents had raised her to be independent but she had still belonged to them. A child needs that connection, that belonging to a family. Now she belonged to Wayne and he belonged to her. They were connected by love and always would be.

Hugs and kisses all around after the service. The little organ continued to fill the chapel with music until they filed out to leave for the restaurant; a private room off of the dining room in the hotel Wind and Sea.

Erin had removed her veil and left it and the bouquet in the car but the little group still turned heads as the four good looking men in navy suits with a flower in their lapels and the two young women in ankle length dresses walked through to the private room. The one in a heavy white lace dress was obviously the bride. The diners applauded. Wayne took Erin's hand and waved to the diners and grinned. Erin blushed but smiled first at them and then at her handsome groom.

The table had a bouquet of pink and white flowers on a white damask cloth. Four silver candlesticks with tall pink candles flanked the flowers. The room was paneled with dark rich paneling and had a soft glow from the candles. Wayne took a deep breath. Wood paneling. Just two hours, he just had to tolerate it for two hours at most. He would have to for Erin's sake. She couldn't have any sense of his concern. He seated his bride and then sat across from her, facing a bank of windows. Sunshine helped. He would try to concentrate on the sun, the food and...that night with Erin.

The luncheon started with a glass of champagne for each and Joel quietly offered the wedding toast and they all touched glasses. The hearty chicken salad, fresh asparagus and rolls had been preordered and were graciously served. Erin felt blessed and tried to cherish each moment. She wouldn't let herself think about 'the boys' leaving in just a few hours. It had been such a happy reunion but so short. She and Wayne would have to fly or drive to San Francisco for a visit soon after their honeymoon. Flying would be best as poor Wayne spent so much of his life driving around the state. Erin looked around at her family and friends. They all felt like family. She looked at her darling husband. Husband, what a wonderful word. She was now a wife. A wife! Wayne's wife! Erin's smile was radiant. She was finally Mrs. Wayne Walters. She would be Mrs. Wayne Walters for the rest of her life. Erin Walters. It sounded so good. She had never been happier and she was sure she would always feel this way.

She reached for Wayne's hand and he looked at her when she took it. He squeezed it as they looked into each other's eyes. Erin had read, in love stories, that a person drowned in her love's eyes. She knew it was real, at this moment she could drown in Wayne's large brown eyes and he seemed to be swimming in hers. Doris looked across at her friend and felt she was intruding. She looked at Joel next to her. He too was watching the couple but looked away quickly and picked up his champagne glass and took a sip. Possibly a silent toast.

Wayne squeezed Erin's hand again and leaned over to give his bride a loving kiss. He wanted nothing more than to be alone with her in their room. They would start their marriage there...here in this hotel. Paul had gotten their bags to the reserved room this morning and tomorrow they would take a shuttle van to the airport. Paul had offered to pick them up but Wayne knew Erin would feel more comfortable if they were not with someone they knew after her wedding night. His precious petite doll. His sensitive, sometimes shy little gal. He would care for her, protect her her entire life and never cause her a moment of pain. He thought of Aunt Mary behind the wall. Was he going to be able to keep this pledge? He closed his eyes and thought a prayer.

A small white wedding cake was carried into the room on a silver tray. The cake was three layers high, large enough for at least ten servings. It was frosted with a white butter frosting and a small bouquet of pink roses and some green leaves covered the top. No plastic bride and groom on this cake. The waiter removed the bouquet and presented it to Erin. At first she held it as she had held hers when walking down the aisle so recently. Then after burying her nose in the fragrance she carefully laid it on the tablecloth above her place setting. The waiter sliced six generous slices of the spice cake with raisins and nuts and placed them on white china dessert plates. Erin smiled at the waiter....it was Wayne's favorite cake and had been kept a surprise. He leaned closer to his wife. "Not a white bride's cake? My favorite? Thanks, it's great." He gave her a gentle kiss and she smiled, grateful that the surprise had pleased him.

Joel looked at his watch. "Oh my gosh, we are going to have to break this up. We hate to eat and run but now that the cake is finished, and we've had a wonderful lunch and lots of champagne, we have to get going if we are to be at the airport an hour early for our flight.

"Darling girl," he said across the table. "You are a beautiful, beautiful bride and I think you have married yourself a great guy. Wayne, I know you will take good care of our sister and you will be a real addition to the family. We now have more reasons to come down to San Diego."

"Oh, Joel. I wasn't enough incentive?"

"Of course 'little bit' but it will be fun watching your happiness as you and Wayne build your lives and we are looking forward to that first niece or nephew."

Erin blushed and tried to laugh.

Jerry also pushed back his chair and stood. "Yes, honey, we

do have to break this up, as much as we hate to. It's been a wonderful time but everything comes to an end." He looked at Paul sitting at his left. I understand you're scheduled to drive us to the airport."

"Yes, Doris, you're going with us, aren't you?"

"I hoped I was to be included although I'm not eager to end this day either."

Joel looked down at his table partner and took her by the arm to help her up. "Of course she is going. We wouldn't have it any other way...would we, Jer?"

"Of course not. How often do we get a lovely young lady to escort us to the airport, or anyplace else, as a matter of fact? Doris, you sit in the back seat with me and Jerry can share the front seat with Paul."

Now it was Doris' turn to blush but she just smiled at Joel and was very aware of his hand on her arm.

Paul hadn't spoken quickly enough but then realized he would have Doris' company on the trip home from the airport and he was thinking of places he could take her. She looked so lovely and was too dressed up to just return to her apartment.

He should have planned ahead for this but he'd had to take over some of Wayne's jobs when Wayne unexpectedly had to go on the road for the full week. Well, no matter. Everything had been accomplished and now that his responsibility as best man was finished, except for the airport trip, he was free to make his own plans for their evening. He couldn't help smiling in anticipation.

Joel saw Paul's smile and guessed his thoughts. "I think Paul will be eager to get rid of us, huh guy?"

"I'd hate to have you miss your plane. There may not be another flight to San Fran. tonight." He smiled at Joel and the four of them moved away from the table.

Wayne pushed back his chair, stood and pulled Erin's chair out for her. "I hadn't realized you would have to leave for the airport quite so soon but I guess Saturday afternoon at the airport can be heavy. Are you leaving from the East or West Terminal?"

"West, unfortunately. It's usually more jammed than the East. It certainly was when we came in."

"Well,...Erin and I can't tell you how much we appreciate your being here this weekend. I know that it meant everything to her." He looked down at his bride who suddenly moved to the brothers and Wayne's best friend.

She put her arms around Jerry and he pulled her to his chest. "We love you, darling girl; be happy." He leaned down and kissed her. Joel came to her for his goodbye then moved to Wayne to shake his hand and give him a sound pat on his back.

"Be happy, darling, that's all we want. We just want you to be happy." Joel took her in his arms and held her close, her head against his chest. Tears began to gather in Erin's eyes and then slowly rolled down her cheeks.

"I can't bear your leaving, not so soon. Your visits are never often enough or long enough since Mom and Dad have been gone. I need you in my life, you know."

"We know honey but now you have Wayne and a whole new life ahead of you. That doesn't mean that we won't come to see you." He looked at Doris. "There are lots of incentives down here we might want to see more often."

Erin laughed through her tears. "Yes I know, like the Wild Animal Park or the Zoo."

"You're right. We haven't seen them often enough." Joel laughed.

Doris felt warm from her toes up and couldn't bring herself to look at him.

Jerry gave Erin another kiss, followed by his brother. "Take care guys, have a wonderful month in Hawaii. Who ever heard of a month's honeymoon? And in Hawaii? Well don't get burned and we'll be looking forward to at least one postcard." The four then left the small dining room to wait for Paul to bring the car to the hotel entrance.

Erin felt too teary to leave the dining room at this moment. The waiter came back with a white cardboard box. "Would you like the rest of the cake saved in this and you don't want to forget your flowers. You are a lovely bride...where were you married?"

"At the Wedding Chapel by the Ocean and yes, we will take the rest of the cake. Thank you." Erin gave the waiter a grateful smile.

"Darling, do you want to take these flowers up to our room?"
.

Erin looked perplexed. "What will we do with them tomorrow? I hate to just leave them in the room to be thrown out after we leave."

"Mrs. Walters, may I make a suggestion?"

"Yes, of course." She smiled up at him. "You are the first person to address me by my new name."

He smiled at the radiant bride. "I'm honored to be the first. You both look so happy and I'd like to wish you years of happiness."

"Thank you, you've already made this meal very special. You have a suggestion about our cake?"

"Yes, there is a young couple, also newlyweds who seem to be on a tight budget. She's in a suit and has a flower on her lapel. They are staying here one night in one of the less expensive rooms. They have ordered a simple dinner and no dessert. If you would want to..."

"Of course...oh thank you for your suggestion. Darling, wouldn't it be lovely to send them the rest of our cake...on plates of course...and the bouquet. We don't really need anymore cake and I do have my wedding flowers in the car. I'm sure Doris will put them in water when she gets home and knowing her will have them all pressed for remembrance."

Wayne gave the glowing face a kiss. "It would be a great idea unless you think they might be offended."

"I don't think they would be offended sir. I could just tell them that another bride and groom wish to share with them."

"Perfect, " Erin said. "I have a feeling you have done this kind of thing before. What is your name?"

"Anthony."

"Well, Anthony, you are more than a waiter. You are obviously a man who enjoys his job and you like to make people happy. I will always remember what you are doing for the other couple. Where are they seated in the dining room? Can we just slip out of here and not be seen? Can you take the cake and flowers to them after we leave?"

"Yes, Mrs. Walters. I will need to get two clean plates for the cake. I don't think they will see you as they are over in the far corner, trying to be by themselves as much as possible. They seem very much in love, just as you are, just on a tighter budget."

"I think we will find ourselves on a budget before we return home. We've saved for a long time for this honeymoon but Hawaii isn't inexpensive, from what I have heard."

"Where are you staying, if I may ask?"

"Pearl City. It' s not the most posh location but less expensive and there is a good beach just beyond the city." Wayne answered. "At least we were told about it." He quickly interjected. "I have reserved a car so we can be free to travel the island."

"It sounds as if you two can have fun where ever you go. Just be careful of that sun. I got so burned in one week I had to spend the second week in bed at our hotel. No fun!"

"Well we wouldn't want that. Thanks for the warning. By the way Anthony, does this hotel offer room service for a light supper?"

"Yes we do and when you're ready for more food just call down and ask for me. I'll be on duty until ten."

"Oh my goodness," Erin said. "I don't think we'll be asking for room service quite that late but I do think it is time we leave here now. You have things to do and I need to get out of this dress."

"Erin!"

She realized what she had said, rather, how it had sounded and blushed again. I didn't mean that. I'm just not used to being this dressed up for this long a time."

Wayne continued laughing but Anthony didn't take the liberty of possibly embarrassing the young bride any more than she had been. He would give them special service and see to it they had a nice supper when they rang for it. He was sure he could find something a little special to slip on their tray. They were a nice, thoughtful couple and he hoped their marriage would be very special.

Chapter 5

Wayne and Erin quietly walked through the dining room to the lobby where they found the bank of elevators. Erin was sure everyone knew she was a bride and knew what was ahead for her; probably more than she did. It made her uncomfortable. She wasn't afraid of this night, just embarrassed that others would know. She had left her bridal bouquet and the veil in the car so she wouldn't be that obvious but her long white dress and the pink rose in Wayne's lapel shouted. 'Just married.' She hoped they could slip into an elevator alone but the hotel was busy and when the first elevator opened in front of them a crowd of tourists pushed them inside and squeezed in after them. At least they were in the back and hopefully the last to leave.

Wayne had to reach past bodies and arms to press the button panel and a few turned to see who was pushing. He pushed number 6 and then leaned back against the wall and took Erin's hand feeling sure he knew how she felt.

Floor 2, a couple got out. Floor 3. Three people got out. Hopefully by the time they reached floor 6 the elevator would be empty except for them. The elevator sailed past floors 4 and 5 and then stopped abruptly at 6. The door slowly opened and Erin took a deep breath. The two couples left had been quiet until the doors opened and then together the four began to sing the wedding march as they walked, two by two off the elevator down the hallway. They all turned to the right still singing. Wayne led Erin to the left and down the hall until they reached another hall where he turned right and stopped in front of a door.

Erin lifted her flushed face to look into her groom's eyes.

"Darling," she whispered. "Our room is the other way. The same way the other couples went."

"I know," he spoke low. "I didn't want them to see which room we had. They might have serenaded us all night." He laughed. "We'll just wait here until we can't hear them any longer and then we'll go find our room."

"Wayne, you are the most thoughtful, darling man I have ever known. Thank you for saving me more embarrassment but, let's just hope someone doesn't come to this room while we are here or worse yet, open the door and catch us standing here."

He quietly laughed and gave her a wink and then left for a moment to check on the merry makers and soon gave Erin the all-clear sign. They quickly retraced their steps past the elevators and then, almost running they found room 602. Wayne already had the card key out ready to put in the lock. After a slight sound they were in and behind a closed door.

The room reflected the ocean with sea blue carpet and matching walls. The furniture, drapes and bedspread were the colors of the surf and sand. A large armoire stood against the wall at the foot of the bed. The open doors exposed a thirty inch television and below it a VCR. Erin wondered how many honeymoon couples had used this room and how many of them would feel the necessity for a movie. She closed the doors and admired the ornately carved wood paneling. Turning, she walked to the windows that covered the outside wall. Sheer white curtains were behind the heavy beige drapes and Erin pulled them aside to look out. The ocean was just across the boulevard. She watched as the lazy waves piled up onto the sand, one after another and then slowly rolled back to regroup and start their journey again.

The sun was still bright in the sky. A sign of the happiness ahead of them, she was sure. A lone airliner was lifting into the sky and heading north. She waved to it. It was probably too early to be Joel and Jerry but she knew it had someone who was headed home or away from their home and she hoped someone would wave a good-bye to 'the boys.'

"Oh Wayne, I just realized that I didn't get to say good-bye to Doris." Erin turned from the window and looked back at Wayne. "She walked out of the room so quickly with Joel, Jerry and Paul we just forgot that we wouldn't see her again for a month. She will be picking up our suitcase with today's clothes after we leave tomorrow but we won't see her."

"Babe, have you ever seen a woman quite so in her seventh heaven as Doris was when she left on Joel's arm with Jerry and Paul close behind her? I don't think she even remembered, at that moment that we were still here. I think she is fast falling for Joel and I wouldn't be surprised if he has just discovered her. At least I hope so. I wouldn't want him to encourage her, as he has this weekend, only to drop her when he gets home. Certainly Paul is in there pitching and she will have his attention here until she discourages him. She's had a weekend she will never forget."

"Wayne. I noticed the attention she was getting but do you really think Joel could be serious about her? My best friend and my brother? Wouldn't that be wonderful! But then Paul is such a sweetheart too. I'm afraid one of them is going to be disappointed and I hate to see that happen."

"Erin. If it's a threesome one has to lose but they are adults and I'm sure can work it out. If Joel is serious and marries her they would live in San Francisco so Paul wouldn't be seeing her frequently as he does now with you. If Paul wins her we will see lots of them but as Joel and Jerry don't come down to San Diego that often, well....when they did come they wouldn't have to see her at all. It will work out. Who knows, she may eventually decide neither of them is the right one for her."

Erin swung away from the window. "Wayne...how can you possibly say she may not pick one of them. They are both wonderful men. How could she find anyone else as wonderful?"

Wayne laughed. "Babe, I think you are just a little bit prejudiced and I don't blame you but you remember that your aunt didn't think I was good enough for you. I just hope for your sake she will eventually change her mind. I know she has hurt you and I will try to see she never hurts you again." His lies were coming more easily but he walked to his bride, gathered her in his arms and closed his eyes to block out vivid memories.

"Wayne, that was the only thing missing today and I tried to not think of Aunt Mary. Everything else was so perfect. We had a perfect wedding and wasn't Anthony a darling!" She looked up at him. "Are you okay?"

"I'm fine, just not sure I'd use that word for him but he was great!" He held her closer as he looked down into her face. "Are you hungry for supper yet?"

"Supper? We just had a fabulous lunch! How can you mention food so soon? I'm not sure I'll ever eat again."

Wayne laughed and kissed her forehead. "Babe, you're always hungry. For such a little bit of a gal I have never understood how you could eat as much food as you do." He kissed her again. "You said you wanted to get out of those clothes. Why don't you use the bathroom first while I organize our suitcases? In fact I can change out here. I'll just change into my pajamas and after you've taken your shower I'll take mine. I'm sure there isn't much room for hanging suits and wedding dresses in there." He let go of her and with a smile she picked up her night bag and headed for the bathroom.

"Wayne...darling, come see this bathroom! It's fabulous! Erin stood in the middle of a large room trying to look at everything at once. A long white marble counter was on the left wall and it had two sinks with ornate gold faucets and handles. A gold tissue box was to the left of the first sink and a white bottle trimmed with gold held liquid soap. A second one was marked. *'Lotion'* in gold. A shower cap and a small bottle of shampoo and a second with conditioner sat on a gold tray. A hair dryer hung on the wall to the left of a full sized mirror that reflected the entire room and a large round magnifying mirror was mounted next to the sink. She would have to have one of those some day...what a wonderful idea. Erin was enthralled with everything she saw.

Two wide steps led down into the largest tub she had ever seen. With it's six jets it was more of a Jacuzzi than a bathtub. Erin stood in awe. At the end of the tub was an over sized glassed-in shower with clear glass. Two large towels hung on heavy gold hooks and a thick white bathmat was draped at the edge of the tub. Erin thought she had never seen such a beautiful bathroom. Two people could easily take showers together or just sit in the immense tub to soak with the jets bubbling water all around them. What fun this would be. She and Wayne would have to do this...but not tonight. She hadn't been with him yet and he hadn't seen her body even in a bathing suit. Her small breasts and boys narrow hips were embarrassing to her and she'd always felt cheated. Her one worry was disappointing Wayne. She knew he would be kind but...how would he really feel?

They had 'petted' as her mother used to describe what nice girls and boys did before they were married. You cuddled and kissed but never...never...went all the way and she hadn't. She stood looking at this magnificent bathroom as Wayne came in.

He had removed his jacket, tie and shirt and she felt a moment of fear as she looked at his bare chest with brown curly hair that went down. at least to his navel. Fear, not from what was to come. She was now a wife. Her body wanted him and she was sure his wanted hers. She was just afraid of disappointing Wayne. Would her boyish body be enough? She had been so enthralled with the room she still stood in the wedding dress that hid her slimness.

"Wayne, oh darling, isn't this the most wonderful bathroom you have ever seen? When we build our own house I want to have one just like it."

Wayne walked around the room feeling impressed but thought it was a little over- done for his taste. Perfect for a bride though. He hadn't told Erin he had splurged and reserved one of the bridal rooms and now he knew the extra expense was worth it. Erin was glowing. He looked down at the heavy bathmat. He knew bathmats. His mother had laid a clean mat next to the tub every night the years she bathed him. God, was this simple move going to bring back more memories? No! He would see that Erin used the mat as he didn't want her to step out onto wet tile on their wedding night. He would always take care of her. She was his life now. The past was the past.

"Pretty impressive, huh, Babe?" He watched her face.

"Oh, it's beautiful. Our room is beautiful but this....this is spectacular!"

"Why don't I draw your bath madam? I'd hate to see you ruin that dress by getting it wet and I don't see a place to hang it."

"Oh yes." Erin put on what she considered a snooty voice. " I'd appreciate it if you 'drew my bath' James...but you're right. I do need to get out of these clothes." She pulled the dress over her head and carried it to the closet where she hung it on a white padded hanger next to two robes. She stood feeling a little exposed in the borrowed long slip as she waited for Wayne to fill the tub and then leave the room. Wayne looked down at the faucet markings. Hot to the left and cold to the right. He turned the handle to the center and felt the water as it came into his hand. More pictures of his mother flashed into his mind. She had always checked the water this way. He wiped his forehead with the back of his wet hand. then looked up into Erin's beautiful blue eyes and took a deep breath as he slowly swallowed. "Do you want a Jacuzzi or a shower madam?"

"Honey, is it okay if I change my mind? I'd like a shower. I think a quick one tonight would be best if we can have a Jacuzzi together tomorrow morning before we leave. That way I could experience both. and I wouldn't get my hair wet."

Wayne turned off the faucets. He would use the shower himself. He'd given up tub baths when he'd left home but a Jacuzzi, especially with Erin wouldn't be the same. It would build new memories. "There's a shower cap on the counter if you want to use it Babe. When you're ready for your shower you'd better adjust the water yourself. I can be 'James' in the morning." Erin giggled at the prospect. "Okay, I'll look forward to it but now you'd better remove yourself so I can get my shower or it will be midnight before you get yours." She gave him a peck and a slight shove. "We can have a bathroom like this one someday, can't we?"

"You will have everything your heart desires my darling even if I have to work two jobs to accomplish it." Erin sobered and turned to him. "No. I'll never make demands like that on you. Never! Never! It's that, well, I've never seen a room like this before. By tomorrow I'll probably think it's too large. How would I ever clean a tub that size? I'd have to climb into it and then crawl around on my hands and knees just to clean the sides. We'll enjoy it tomorrow and then let someone else worry about cleaning it." She laughed up at him and loved the feel of his bare chest in her arms.

Chapter 6

Wayne wore navy cotton pajama pants and his body was still damp from his shower. He hadn't washed his heavy thick hair as he didn't want it wet when he held Erin. Tomorrow would be time enough when they frolicked in the spa tub, jets going full tilt. They could shampoo in the suds. Wayne took a deep breath as he looked at his bride. She stood in front of the drawn sheer drapes...the glow of a setting sun seemed to surround her. She wore a long pale pink satin gown that clung to her body. Tiny thin straps held up the neckline. Her breasts were small smooth round mounds just below the straps. Wayne could visualize soft pink nipples cresting her breasts. Her waist was small and her belly was just a slight break in the smooth gown as it fit over her slim hips. He hadn't been with a woman before and he was eager to find what lay just below the swell.

Memories of his mother...after his bath...dressing him in a little girl's pair of cotton panties with lace around the legs then a cotton dress with a tiny rosebud print. She would brush his hair and spray a little rose water on him and then send him to his father. His father would always be sitting on the edge of his bed, the bed he shared with his mother. He would smile at Wayne, beckon to him and then hold out his arms.

The first time he was only four and didn't understand what was happening. He had sensed his parents had wished for a girl so he had to fill in for her. The first time his mother had stood in the bedroom doorway watching as his father slowly pulled down the snowy white panties. Then he gently pulled the dress off over his head and then the slip. as he stood quietly in front of his father with the panties down around his ankles. His father turned him around and laid him face down on the bed. First he put his face on his round bottom and his tongue explored between his crack. A movement of resisting and he had a sound smack across his head. He learned to quietly take what was done...what became a ritual every day. After the tongue Wayne remembered being put on his hands and knees on the bed and first his father's fingers would explore and stretch his bottom and then something large and hard would press and push until it was inside of him. In and out it would go until his father made weird sounds and his bottom would feel wet and sticky. Tears would quietly cover his face as he muted his sobs in the covers. When he finally was allowed to leave the room again he saw that his mother had watched the whole thing. His shame and the fact that his mother had prepared him for the father and had allowed his terrible pain from the tearing did something to him he never recovered from. She would then take him to the bathroom to wash the blood and the other stuff off and would tell him how much he had pleased his father, therefore pleasing her.

When twelve he stood in front of his father and realized he was looking him eye to eye and that day he said. "Never Again!" His father left their home two days later and his mother never forgave him. Him, not the father. When he displeased her she would beat him with a strap. Never where the bruises could be seen but on the softest part of his body. He would be deprived of food and as money was scarce he had no way to buy any for himself. When she went out he was locked in a closet sometimes with his hands and feet bound with duct tape. His mouth had even been bound occasionally if she was gone for long periods so he couldn't call for help. They lived beyond the outskirts of Pearl City in Hawaii and had few neighbors and almost no friends. He hadn't had schooling beyond sixth grade except the training of repairing cars his father had given him.

The rest he had taught himself. One boy had befriended him. Tony Barcino, but Wayne never told him of the abuse he got from his parents. Shame kept him from talking about it and fear of being put in a children's home or even worse. His mother always threatened him with worse punishments if he told so he had learned to accept while he secretly made plans how, when he was older, he would escape. He had never even dreamed of fighting back...of possibly hurting his mother. He just took his 'punishment.'

Erin watched his face as he looked at her. He looked so strained. As if his thoughts were far away. "Wayne, honey? Do I look all right?"

"You are the most beautiful thing I have ever seen. I just have to stand here and stare to be able to remember for the rest of my life how you look right now." He would never tell Erin, or anyone else, the abuse he had taken as a child and he would never allow another child to be mistreated if he could possibly prevent it.

"God was good when he brought you to me. I will look up his commandments and never again disobey even one." Tears filled his eyes. "I'm so blessed to have you, Erin. You will never know how blessed I am."

He went to her and enfolded her little body against his. He covered her elfin-like face with kisses. Her little pointed chin, high cheekbones and the incredible blue eyes. He kissed the lids and the lashes as her tears began to fall.

"Darling, I'm the one who is blessed. I love you with my whole being. I was a little afraid of tonight but now I'm not. You know this is my first time and I'm sure you...like most men have had other girls, although you have never mentioned it to me. I know you will be gentle but I want so much to please you."

"Erin," he breathed in her ear. "I'm...a virgin just as you are so we will learn together. I want you to enjoy it as much as I will but I'm concerned because I've heard it might be a little painful for you...this first time. I'll try to be careful. I don't want to hurt you." He wiped her tears with his fingers and held her closer.

She could feel how much he wanted her and she melted closer to him. He picked her up in his arms and carried her the few feet to the large bed where he laid her down and while still holding her stretched out,...pulling the sheet to cover their bodies.

Chapter 7

The next morning Erin awakened to see Wayne watching her. "Hi, did you sleep?" She said softly.

"Yes, but are you okay? Did I hurt you?"

Erin crawled into the fold of an arm and his other one went around her. "I'm wonderful. I feel like a complete woman for the first time in my life. I am really yours now as I have been a part of you."

Wayne felt beyond emotions. He had never been this happy. He said nothing but just held her with his lips on her face. The experience had been beautiful and he had felt something his father never could have felt with him. What a poor sad creature he was. What a sick man and yes, his mother had also been sick. Even when young he had somehow known that this joining with another man was not for him but he might never have had this joy if he hadn't met Erin. He didn't know how to pray but he knew there was a higher power out there somewhere taking care of him. He had survived the terrible years and he had survived Aunt Mary. She would never destroy their life together. He prayed for forgiveness for his sins but then hadn't he been sinned against? Transgressed. He thought the word was transgressed. Yes, they had transgressed against him and wasn't that one of God's laws? He had heard preachers talk about this and now he asked to be delivered from evil. He looked at Erin. He'd been delivered from evil and he thanked God with all of his heart. He held Erin closer and he felt himself begin to respond to her body.

"You know what? If we don't get up right now we will never have our bubbly bath in that big bathtub you love so much and we will never make our plane."

Erin rubbed her body on his and his excitement rose. "I'm wondering if I care if we have that Jacuzzi or not. I'm not even sure if I care about making our plane if we can just stay like this all day...right here making love over and over and over."

He gave her a squeeze. "I'd love nothing more darling but I think your body should get some rest before we make love again." He closed his eyes as he remembered the pain when his father would repeat and repeat his act. No, he wouldn't do that to Erin as much as he wanted her.

"I feel fine Wayne, honestly I do. I would love to make love again, right now."

"Me too but let's go play in that big tub. I've never had a little elf in my bath before. Also, you know we never did call Anthony last night and I'll bet he didn't have to wonder why."

Erin blushed and he realized he could have avoided that comment. "Sorry, I should have said I'm getting a little hungry...for food, aren't you? I do think we need some before we get on our plane."

The sheet suddenly flew off both of them as Erin bounced off of the bed and headed to the bathroom. She closed the door after herself but in a few minutes she was again at the bedside. "The water is running and the plug is closed. You use the bathroom and I'll get our wedding clothes packed for Doris to pick up. Just let me know when the water is deep enough for the bubbles."

Wayne rolled off his side of the bed and stood in the middle of the room. Their night clothes had been discarded during the night and now as husband and wife they stood naked, looking at each other. Erin didn't look away but went to him and held her body next to his as they had in the darkness of the night.

"Now, my darling I am truly your wife just as Eve was to Adam and we will never need fig leaves to cover ourselves."

She laughed. "Well, there might be a few exceptions."

Wayne gave her a long loving kiss, slowly tasting her lips, and then gave her bottom a little slap and taking her arm, pulled her into the bathroom and helped her down the steps into the hot water. Their bodies soon slithered together in the softened water and the jet's bubbles. They were like innocent children in their joy.

Chapter 8

The dining room was only half full when they arrived for a late breakfast. Erin was wearing stone-washed blue jeans, jacket, white tee shirt and tennis shoes. She had a long silver chain with her mother's locket around her neck and silver earrings. Wayne was also in jeans with a white dress shirt, opened at the neck with cuffs rolled up to just below his elbows and white deck shoes. They no longer looked like a bride and groom but as tourists ready to see San Diego. Anthony greeted them and led them to one of his tables. He made no comment about their having missed their dinner but would give them a surprise this morning with their breakfast. He started to ask if they had slept well, a question he often asked his guests but realized it wouldn't be tactful for newlyweds so he just said good morning and asked for their order.

Erin looked at the long menu and settled on a very special eggs Benedict and Wayne, not sure what it was, ordered the same. Orange juice and coffee were the chosen beverages.

"Excuse me but may I ask a personal question?"

Erin looked up a little apprehensively.

"Do you two drink alcohol in the morning?"

Erin grinned in relief and Wayne admitted they had once in a while but why the question?

I would just like to bring you something for the occasion, if that's all right and you trust me. And, you might like to know that the other newlyweds were very touched with your kindness last night. They enjoyed the cake and she was very pleased to have the flowers. I sent a vase to their room so she could put the bouquet in water during the night."

"Anthony, you are a very special person and we trust you

completely so bring whatever you have in mind."

Erin smiled at the two men and was eager to see what the 'special thing' would be for them.

Anthony returned to the table with a tray and two tall tapered glasses of orange juice. "I thought you should have a little champagne this morning so I put it in your orange juice so the other guests won't get the wrong idea about you. If you can handle a second it will be ready in a moment now that I have opened the bottle." He smiled as if very pleased with himself.

Erin and Wayne laughed and Erin clapped her hands with delight. "What a sweetie you are. What a perfect thing to start our long trip." she said.

"Please be sure to put it on our bill and thank you for thinking of it."

Anthony left smiling and then quickly returned with their hot plates of eggs Benedict with slices of an orange arranged along the side of each plate.

He then brought two steaming cups of coffee. "Is there anything you would like me to put in your coffee?" He asked with a grin.

"I have a feeling you are not referring to cream or sugar but no. I think Erin and I will drink our coffee very black this morning. We do have to be very sober to check in with Delta and to make our plane." Wayne grinned.

"I believe you said you were leaving for Hawaii this morning. Have either of you been there before?"

"Yes we leave at twelve forty three and no, we haven't been there before." Erin said.

"I have, a couple of times but for very short stays."

Erin looked at Wayne. "I didn't know that. What part of Hawaii were you in?"

"Waikiki, I went with a friend from work to try surfing. We

quickly found it wasn't our thing in those waves."
"Honey, I didn't know you surfed. Are we going to be repeating things you did and saw with your friend on this trip? We should have chosen a completely new spot for our honeymoon. Someplace neither of us had been before."
"Don't worry, Mrs. Walters. Hawaii will seem like an entirely different place with you along and besides...a man likes to be able to show his wife around places. I know you will have fun there. Well, enjoy your breakfast. Let me know if there is anything else you would like. "
With that statement and a smile Anthony left them and went to take care of other guests. They didn't see him again until he returned to give them their bill on a silver tray.
Wayne checked the bill carefully. "Would you believe he didn't bill us for the drinks?"
"Oh darling. can you give him a big tip? We can economize some place else. He has been so wonderful to us both last night and now."
"I agree. I did tip him yesterday but he has made this stay so special. Would twenty dollars be all right?"
"I think it would be perfect if he doesn't have to pay for the champagne but I guess we will never know. I think Anthony will be pleased with twenty."
"Then this should take care of everything." Wayne said as he placed the bill and the money on the tray. "Shall we go?"
Wayne pulled out her chair, took her arm and as they left the dining room they turned to look back at Anthony. They smiled as he grinned and gave a little nod of his head as if wishing them well.
Their baggage was at the check-out desk; The bag with their wedding clothes was separate but well marked for Doris. Wayne stood in line to check out and had finished about the

time a porter came to the desk to announce the airport van was at the door. He placed their luggage on his cart and Wayne and Erin followed. Their wonderful experience at the Wind and Sea was over but their flight to Hawaii was the start of a new one.

Chapter 9

The 12:43 flight left the gate on time. It was a seven hour flight to Honolulu and they would have a cold drink and peanuts soon after they took off and dinner before landing. They settled down in their seats just behind the wing and Erin looked around at the other passengers. She wondered if 'newlywed' was written all over them. Did everyone know they had made love for the first time last night? She was feeling paranoid and would have to get over it. Of course it didn't show!

"Excuse me, would you like a cold drink or maybe you would like a little champagne?"

Erin looked into the smiling eyes of the attendant. "How did you know?" she asked in a whisper. "Do we have signs on our backs?"

The flight attendant laughed. "No sign but when you have been on as many flights to Hawaii as I have you can usually spot newlyweds. Were you married last night?"

Erin blushed in spite of herself. "Yes, yesterday morning and we're going to have a month in Hawaii."

"That's wonderful. Usually the couples just have a few days or a week at most. A month... will you be able to get to some of the other islands?"

"I don't think so. We'll just spend our time in Honolulu. I'm sure we will find plenty to do. We have already been warned about being in the sun too much." She laughed self consciously. Next she would be telling her life's story to this stranger. This wasn't like her at all...but being nervous seemed to make her more talkative. Wayne was sitting watching her and listening with amusement. He was so proud to have her as his bride he could shout it from the rooftops or at least all through this large plane but that would upset Erin so he just sat and enjoyed the conversation.

The attendant stooped down and took two 'splits' of champagne from the cooler then gave them two plastic glasses and some peanuts. "Enjoy your flight and Hawaii and...congratulations."

"Thanks." Erin said, smiling at the woman and feeling more in control.

Wayne opened the bottles, poured the golden liquid into the glasses and they touched their glasses in a salute to each other. Wayne leaned over to kiss Erin and then they sat and slowly sipped the lovely beverage.

They'd had a late evening and an early morning. The Jacuzzi had been worth it but the hours, the hot water, the big breakfast and the hum of the plane engines, as well as the champagne, all acted like a sleeping pill and Wayne dozed with Erin's head on his shoulder until it was almost time for their supper. In just a few hours they would be arriving in Honolulu and after getting their baggage they would find the car rental and take off to their Pearl City motel. It would be late but they could sleep in. They had no special plans for tomorrow and a whole month ahead of them.

All had gone smoothly although the drive to Pearl City had seemed to take forever. In spite of their long naps on the plane they were once again ready for sleep. Wayne pulled their car in front of an old motel, the kind that was popular thirty or more years ago. The description Wayne had been given by one of the other salesmen was deceiving. 'Beach homes.' He knew there would be separate cottages, all with kitchens. next to a main office. But this?

The sleepy attendant gave them their key for unit 3 without

much conversation. The description was right but even in the dark he could see that the place was in need of repair and paint. He looked at Erin and took a deep breath as he put the key in the lock and opened the front door. Wayne felt for the light switch and finally found it on what felt like a wood wall. The light blazed from a single light bulb in the center of the ceiling. Wayne froze. The entire room was paneled with knotty pine. The knot twisted in his middle.

He could hear Aunt Mary laughing at him.

Erin walked into the middle of the room, looking around.

"We can't stay here Erin. No way can we stay here. Not after what we had last night am I going to let you stay here."

"It isn't so bad darling. It will be a new adventure. One we can laugh about with our children." She walked around the room. "I'm not surprised it was so affordable."

"We will stay tonight Babe, but tomorrow we will go back to Waikiki and find someplace better. I'm sure there will be an opening somewhere. You will not spend your honeymoon here."

"Honey, we could spend a week here. You had talked about the great uncrowded beaches that are near here and we can visit the memorials. It's best to see them while we are so close. I know it's different from last night but I know you splurged on a honeymoon room. No! Before you say anything. I saw the bill when you were paying. I never thought I could love you more than I did last night but I do. Anyplace with you will be wonderful. This will be like our first home, a modest start but, darling, I really don't mind."

Wayne took Erin in his arms and then held her small face in his hands and looked into her blue eyes. "We'll stay long enough to see the memorials and the beach but then we will move. We will be out most of the day and we can buy our meals so you won't have to cook here. I wouldn't trust the dishes and you're not going to spend your honeymoon scrubbing the place as well as the pots and pans. We will even have breakfast out. God knows what germs are running around here." Wayne looked around what to him was a terrorizing room and said. "Let's see about the bedroom. If the sheets are clean we can stay for a few days."

Erin walked into the bedroom. More paneling and no window. At night it seemed like a dark hole and with no window it would probably be the same during the day. She pulled back the thin spread and then the sheet. They looked clean. as did the pillows.

Wayne pushed down on the mattress. It was thin but they would survive. Having Erin with him might help him to survive the knotty pine and the terrible feeling of guilt and fear that was building within. He moved into the bathroom. The towels and wash clothes looked clean and smelled of disinfectant. The sink and toilet were old and stained but clean. A small shower head was against one wall showing above the shower rod and a stiff plastic shower curtain with a pattern of large Hawaiian flowers and leaves was pulled almost covering the tub. Showers would be necessary but he was a little uncomfortable about what he would find when he opened the curtain. How recently had it been cleaned? There was no way he would let Erin sit in bath water in this tub. There would be no water frolicking together except in the ocean waves.

Chapter 10

Wayne opened his eyes to almost total darkness. He turned to look at the small clock radio that was on the single nightstand next to their double bed. Eight o'clock. My God, how could it be that late, but then they hadn't gone to bed until after eleven thirty and they'd had a long day. He could see into the living dining area and the kitchen and realized light was streaming into that single room. It was only this windowless bedroom that was dark. He wondered what was behind these walls, wondered if they had covered a window or if it was something outside they didn't want seen. and decided he would check them out after their breakfast. Maybe earlier would be a better idea, before Erin was up.

He slowly pulled the sheet back so as to not waken her. He sat on the edge of the bed for a few minutes trying to determine where his suitcase was. Erin's was on a straight backed chair...his was on the floor next to it. He slowly lifted from the bed and went to his suitcase and opening it, felt until he found his denim shorts and a tee shirt. He would worry about a shower and clean underclothes later. For now he just wanted to walk around this 'palace' they had rented for the month.

Wayne quietly opened the outside door and went into the sunshine and the tropic air. California air was warm but not like this. It brought back memories. About the only good childhood memory of Hawaii. He took deep breaths. Such a relief after the stifling musty rooms. There had to be an air conditioner even in such an ancient rental. It was one thing they hadn't checked for last night. It would be the first thing he would check when he was finished checking the outside. It reminded him of the house he was raised in but it had had two ceiling fans. Last night they had checked in, put their suitcases in the bedroom, taken their night clothes from the overnight bag and had fallen into bed. The one delightful surprise was the bed was only a double. He suspected they were hard to find now with all of the popular queen and king sized beds. The double bed encouraged 'spooning.' Cuddling so that their bodies fit.... a front to a back. He suspected they hadn't turned often during the night as they had both slept soundly. He'd wakened holding Erin and she hadn't moved when he had turned to check the time. Holding Erin every night and making love is what he could look forward to. He smiled as he walked around the buildings.

One wall of their bedroom was against what he had suspected, the next unit. The other walls overlooked a row of buildings with large signs promoting nude dancing. Above were multi colored fluorescent lights. A navy town. Of course! Damn! How could he have been directed to this place for their honeymoon? Well, that settled it. They would see the monuments for the attack on Pearl Harbor, which started World War Two. They would go to a couple of the beaches and that would be it! He would not subject Erin to flashing neon lights and possibly rowdy sailors. That isn't what he wanted her to remember about this month

Walking back in the dry dirt he looked forward to a shower and wondered if he could take one before Erin woke up. Better yet, he would check out the bathroom to see if the shower was large enough for two. A great way to start a day. If it wasn't clean he would scrub it.

Erin was standing at the kitchen counter when he entered the cottage. "Where did you go? I was worried"

"I'm sorry I worried you Babe, you were asleep and I was wondering why the bedroom and bath don't have windows. What they were covering up?"

"What did you find? Is it something horrible?"
"Yeah. Strip Bars with flashing neon lights, day and night."
"Oh, Wayne no, you're kidding me." She looked into his face.
"Wish I was and I'm even more determined that we are going to leave here. I will agree to a few days for seeing the war memorials and we can hit a couple of beaches but then we leave. We won't bother to buy food for cooking. I'm taking you out for every meal we are here. I don't trust this place. It sure isn't what I planned for our honeymoon."
"We could make do but if we can find something else in our budget I'll be willing to go. Can we get our showers and then find some breakfast? I think I'd like to see the Pearl Harbor memorials. I'd like that to be the first thing we see here. Does that sound all right to you?"
"I was thinking about our shower when I was outside. First, is it large enough for two and is it clean? That I will check out before you go in there."
Erin laughed and gave Wayne a strong hug. I've already checked out the bathroom. There is a bathtub with a shower head at the end. Do you think we could have fun with that?"
Wayne let go of Erin but grabbed her hand. "We can have fun with anything. Cum- mon. I'll get the water going and then I'll beat you into that tub."
Erin gave a little shriek as she pulled away from him and started pulling off her pink nightgown. She already had the advantage as he was fully dressed even down to his shoes. At least she thought he was until he pulled off his shirt and then his shorts and saw he was naked. He quickly flipped off his tennis shoes and ran into the bathroom, pulling the shower curtain back as he leaned over to turn on the water. Erin came up behind him and leaned her body over his. Wayne almost went into the

tub head first but turned around gabbing her, and picking up the small frame in his arms, carried her into the bedroom. The cold water running from the tap became hot and the bathroom soon steamed like a thick fog.

Wayne and Erin lay in the center of the bed. Even in the stifling room they lay with their arms around each other...their bodies close.

"That wasn't fair, you know. You took advantage of my awkward position."

"I know." Erin giggled. "Wasn't it delicious?"

"Delicious is the word for it, also steamy. We steamed up the living room window." He nuzzled his face into her neck and then suddenly looked up. "Oh, my God! The bath water!" Wayne pulled away from Erin, rolled off the bed and ran into the bathroom. He quickly turned off the faucets and then sat on the edge of the tub in the fog laughing.

"Erin, anyone going past this cottage now will know we are honeymooners who are very much in love."

Erin, in embarrassment, pulled the sheet over her head and laughed into her pillow.

Wayne slowly left the bathroom, laid down on top of the shaking sheet and put his arm across Erin's body. "Let's get dressed and out of here before we get into trouble again."

Erin pulled the sheet down, uncovering her face. "Trouble! You call what we just did trouble?"

"No darling, but I suspect there won't be anymore hot water in this entire unit for hours. I'll take a cold shower. I think I need it. They both started laughing and Wayne took the little face in his hands again and kissed it. "Cum mon, we have to leave this place. We need fresh air. It's hot out, so dress light." He pulled the sheet from her and she tried to cover her body and then suddenly jumped from the bed and bent over her suitcase to choose her days clothes.

Wayne turned from the sight...shocked at his reaction from seeing her little bottom in that position. He was trying so hard to put all of that behind him. Would he ever be allowed to forget? Damn his father...intruding even on his honeymoon. He picked up his clothes from the living room floor and went into the bathroom. He would get a pair of clean white under shorts from his suitcase after the shower. Erin followed him into the bathroom. "I think I can stand a cold shower if you wouldn't mind some company."

Wayne didn't answer but just held out his arms to her as she climbed into the tub.

Erin slipped into bikini underpants and a bra in a matching light blue plaid. Wayne wondered if this was her normal wear or honeymoon clothes. She pulled on jean shorts and a pink tee shirt, picked up pink sandals but thought better of it and pulled her tennis shoes from under the bed where they had landed last night. and sat on the bed to put them on.

"Wayne, honey, are you all right? You have become so serious and quiet."

"I'm fine, Babe. I guess I'm just eager to get out of this musty place and find us some breakfast. I know there are lots of fast food places around here." He looked quickly at Erin. "We'll get away from the strip joints. We can eat and then head for the memorials and I promise you a nice lunch."

Breakfast at Sizzler's. They found they were hungrier than they had thought. The small dinner on the plane had been so many hours ago. Waffles, sausage, hash browns, juice and coffee had calmed the pangs and it was nice sitting in an air conditioned restaurant in a secluded booth. They didn't need other people now.

"I love you, Erin Walters."

"I love you too, Wayne Walters and I love my new name. Thank you for giving it to me. I think I'd like a tablet so I can sit and write Erin Walters, over and over and over."

"You will have plenty of reasons to write that name during the next years. How are you at paying bills?"

"No, you wouldn't do that to me?"

"You don't want to handle our household accounts, pay the rent and our taxes?"

"Oh, I hope you're not serious." She looked at him with almost fright in her eyes.

"Babe, that really worries you?"

"Yes. I have always been terrible in math. That was one thing I didn't have to worry about in my job. There isn't much math. Besides, I have always felt it is the man's responsibility to pay the bills. My father always did it. He would give mother money for the weeks food bills and incidentals. He would write the checks for the mortgage, electricity, water, etc. I pay my rent now and I budget my paycheck every month but darling, I hate it. My check book is always a little off so I just round out the amount to what the bank says I have.

If I thought I had to balance your money too...oh Wayne, please, you will handle our finances, won't you?"

He laughed. "I'll take care of all of the finances if it will make you happy. Don't ask me to do algebra or trig. but simple math I can do. There really won't be that much of a change for me. I'm moving into your apartment so our light and water bills may be a little higher and the food bill but other than that things should be about the same. Do you want to keep your own checking account as you have it now?"

"Do I have to?"

"No, we can get a joint account when we get back and we'll figure out between our two salaries what we have for the monthly bills and what we have for clothes and other things. Does that sound okay?"

"It sounds wonderful. You're my man and I'll love your taking care of me. I realize this isn't the way the 'modern' woman thinks but I'll love it."

"That will be about the happiest thing I have done in my life."

She started to give him a kiss but the waitress was suddenly at their booth with their check in hand. "It looks as if everything is all right. How was the food?" She smiled at them. "When did you fly in?"

"Last night." Wayne said.

"You staying close to here?"

"No, we're at the Pearl City Motel. It was recommended to me by a friend in San Diego "

"Recommended by a friend? He must have seen it years ago. How long are you planning on being here? That place has changed these past five years."

"We're staying a month and we realized it must have changed. It isn't what we had expected."

"You don't plan to stay here in Pearl City the entire time, do you?"

"We had planned on it but changed our minds when we saw the motel. We want to see the sights here in the city, the memorials and such and then we want to go to some of the beaches for a day or two but then we plan to leave for Waikiki. We hope to find a place within our months budget there. Have any recommendations?"

"There are hostels but I have a feeling you guys want a private room. There's a place in Honolulu called the Pale Pua Nui. It's an older four-story building with studio apartments. It would be cheaper if you could cook some of your meals and this place gives discounts if you stay more than two weeks. There is some parking available for about $5.00. I think it would cost you about $44 a day this time of year. Would that be in your budget?"

"Yes, oh yes, we can manage that. We saved for this hon...we saved for this trip so that would be fine. We knew Hawaii wouldn't be cheap so we really appreciate this help."

"That sounds good, Miss. is there a phone book I can look at? I'd like to see if we can get a reservation." Wayne interjected.

The waitress smiled. "I can do even better than that. I have a business card at the counter because my sister works there. I wouldn't recommend it if it wasn't clean and well maintained. There isn't any air conditioning but they have good ceiling fans and the beach is only about five minutes. Give me a minute and I'll get a card for you. Better yet, why don't you come up to the desk and I'll give you the card and you can use the phone over there in the corner. Tell them Margie from the Sizzler in Pearl City told you about them. It might help."

"Thanks, I'll do that." Wayne said as he took the card and walked to the phone.

"Honeymooners, huh.?"

"Oh gosh. Does it show that much?"

"Relax hon. It doesn't show that much. I just couldn't help but notice the kisses. You are obviously very much in love and it's always great to see. My husband and I were in love like you but we only had eight years."

"Oh, I'm sorry."

"Yeah, me too. We were navy and I guess you have to be prepared for that possibility. We had lots of navy friends so I have stayed here where I get more support than I would have in Minnesota. Besides, I like the weather, even in the summer."

Margie leaned closer to Erin. "I've met a new guy and I think it's gonna take. He's pretty great. Different from Ron but great and he loves me." She paused. "How long you been married?"

"I thought that showed too. We were married day before yesterday in San Diego. We had a small wedding in a beautiful little chapel but it was lovely." Erin wasn't about to tell Margie about their honeymoon room and the big bathtub, even though she was tempted. Women do tell other women, even perfect strangers, many things about their personal lives but Margie had lost her first love and was hoping to find happiness with a second. They might not be able to afford a honeymoon suite so she wouldn't flaunt her beautiful romance and what she and Wayne had. She would just hope that the second man would give Margie even half of the happiness she was feeling even with the Pearl Harbor Motel. She was right. They would be laughing about this experience in the future.

Wayne came up to the two women with a big smile on his face. "We are in luck, thanks to Margie here. They have an opening, a unit with a kitchenette and we can have it for three weeks and we do get a discount. Providence must have led us to you, Margie. We had a great breakfast, met you and now we have a new place to stay and we move in on Saturday. We'll be back here for breakfast and possibly other meals while we're here in Pearl City. I don't want Erin cooking in our present place."

"From what I've heard I don't blame you. I'll be looking forward to seeing both of you again. The visitor center at the USS Arizona is open until five P.M. That and the Bowfin Park. Why don't you spend the rest of your time here on the beaches. We do have lovely white sand and the beaches aren't as populated as they are in Waikiki. You'll find them along highway 93 going north from here."

"You've been wonderful but I'm afraid we've taken up too much of your time from your other customers. We'll see you later and thanks for all of your help, Margie." Erin held her hand for a moment and then Wayne shook it firmly. "Yeah, thanks for the help. We'll be back." Margie watched the young couple leave the restaurant and get into a car parked near the entrance. "Lord, please give me another love like that. Amen!"

Chapter 11

Just eight feet down. There she sat. The USS Arizona. Erin looking down at the ship felt overcome with the drama of what had happened that day in December. 1941. She looked at the pass between the mountains where the Japanese planes had flown to Pearl Harbor. She looked around trying to visualize the harbor full of ships being bombed and the town being bombed. People running. people dying...so many young men.

"Wayne," she said softly. "My great uncle was in command of a hospital ship here in the harbor when the bombing started. He had to get the ship out into the open sea but also picked up as many survivors as he could. I grew up hearing his stories about it.. I have always wanted to see this. It's so hard to believe. Nineteen, their average age. Just kids. So many younger than I am. When will man's inhumanity to man ever end?"

Wayne put his arm around her shoulder. "You have never told me that story before. I didn't know you had family who had been here during the bombing. I'm sure this is much more emotional for you because of it. Did your uncle survive?"

"Yes, he lived until he was 74. With newer wars you don't hear about World War 2 very much. I wouldn't be surprised if it isn't even taught in schools. I know some schools are trying to convince students there never was a holocaust. Can you imagine our country being in the center of two large wars at the same time? I pray we never have another. Look down there darling. 1177 young men are down there. Oh, this gives me the chills. I think I've seen enough. I feel so for their families...for their loved ones. Death is bad enough but violent death....no one should have to suffer violent death."

Aunt Mary! God! Oh God! Wayne thought. Her death hadn't been like this. It was quick but he was the one who couldn't escape that violent horror. A chill went through him.

They slowly walked from the water grave working their way through the crowds. She hadn't wanted to read the names on the Arizona's bell. She would silently say prayers for all those who were killed but she didn't want to see pictures or read names. She still didn't know many Japanese people. Some individuals she knew were delightful but a deep hate and resentment for the leaders of the Japanese government still sat in her heart. Her grandparents often talked, long after the war and after the Korean and Vietnam wars, about how we had paid to rebuild Japan and now they were stabbing us in the back by stealing our plans and underselling our products to the world. Germans were the other people her grandparents hated. She was so young when she was first aware of their discussions of the wars. They hated our government for getting our men into the Vietnam and Korean wars. Politics. They felt it was all because of politics and greed for money. At the dinner table they would talk about Roosevelt. They had always been Democrats until Roosevelt---'sold our country down the river' at Malta. They were very sure of this.

Then it was the cold war with the Russians. Her mother talked about living under a fear of another war during her younger years. How she wished her parents could be with her now. How she wished they could live now when there was no war. Internal fights in countries but no big war. She wasn't sure it would last but was loving the feeling of peace. She had been a late-in-life child. Wanted, but a real surprise, several years after her brothers who had also come along later than most marrieds started their families. They were not a 'young' family but an 'old family' because her folks were not interested in children's games or interests so they were raised on politics and wars. Now she wasn't interested in politics and certainly she didn't want to talk or be any part of a war. This had been interesting but she had seen enough.

"Erin, how about seeing the Bowfin Park?"

"What is that? I'm not sure I know what it is."

"It has a World War Two sub there and a museum about how subs were developed through the years, I think from the turn of the century. You might find it interesting. Do you remember your folks or grandparents talking about the Japanese kamikaze pilots? Very few people knew they also had a suicide torpedo. A torpedo with a single seat and a volunteer, just like with the planes, sat in it and were blasted off and they piloted it to it's target."

"I had heard about the kamikaze pilots but a torpedo? Were any ships hurt by these?" "They know about one. the USS Mississinewa. Would you like to see one of the torpedos and the sub?"

"Darling." Erin said softly. "Have you seen them?"

Wayne hesitated and then said "Yes." He had admitted to having been at Waikiki but not here. He hoped she wouldn't pick up on it but he couldn't lie to her.

"Would you mind terribly if we passed on it?"

"No, of course not. I want you to see only what pleases you. There is a Hawaiian Plantation Village you might like to see. It isn't far from here."

"That sounds like more fun. Let's try it."

"Great, we can see the village and then have lunch. Do you want to try to hit a beach today? We still have what, three, four days to fill before we go to Waikiki." Wayne laughed. "What day is this?"

Erin laughed. "I think it's only Monday."

"Monday? We were married yesterday? My God, that doesn't seem possible."

"Honey, no, we were married Saturday. We had our wedding night in San Diego then the next day, yesterday, Sunday, we flew to Honolulu. We drove here, went to bed and woke up this morning. Monday." She laughed. "We had breakfast at Sizzler's and had that nice waitress who found us another place to stay, this time in Waikiki. Then we drove out here and now, here we are."

Erin looked at Wayne. "Honey, it isn't like you to be this confused. You haven't been yourself today and I'm worried about you. Is there anything I can do to help?"

"Help? There isn't anything that needs helping. I guess we've been pushing ourselves this weekend. I've loved every minute but we have been moving so fast I've just lost track of time. I'll admit I have been upset about our honeymoon palace. We have Tuesday, Wednesday, Thursday and then Friday before we can move to the other place Saturday morning. How are we going to fill those days without driving into Honolulu, which we can do. It's just that we have three more weeks to see that end of the island."

"Wayne, how would it be if we go to a beach now and save the plantation until tomorrow?"

"Is that what you'd like to do?"

"I really am eager to get to a beach. I've never been in a warm ocean or on white sands. Would you mind too much if we changed our plans? Wouldn't there be a hot dog stand near the beach so we could have lunch there? Then we could lie on the beach until time to get cleaned up for dinner, have dinner and ..." She smiled. "We could go to bed."

"You don't want to stay out of that place longer? It's going to be hot and stuffy."

Erin felt hurt, rejected. "We survived last night and I was looking forward to tonight." Erin looked down. "I hoped you would be feeling the same."

"Of course I do. It's just not the place I had thought we would have. I guess I'm disappointed for you. I wanted it to be so perfect."

"Wayne, it's our honeymoon, nothing could hurt that...except our attitude." She looked at him. "Let's go back and get into our suits, grab towels and sunscreen then find a nice, quiet beach." She held his arm and watched his face, still feeling a little rejected. The crowds at the memorial were beginning to push past them. It was crowded, noisy!

"You're right sweetheart. Let's get out of here. We can come back earlier tomorrow, hopefully before the crowds. The plantation opens at 8:00." Wayne smiled. "Not that I think we will be up that early." He looked at her with what he hoped was a wicked smile and got a poke in the ribs so he must have been successful. Erin felt happier.

"Come on, let's go back to the car." Wayne took Erin's hand as they left.

The motel didn't look any better in the daytime. Wayne unlocked their door and held it open for Erin. The oppressive heat hit her in the face but she didn't say a word about it. "Look, there is a fan in the ceiling...why didn't we notice it before? This should help move the air around. I don't think the steam bath we gave the rooms this morning helped." She laughed at the memory.

There are screens on the windows but I'd hate to open them because of the dirt driveway. Any wind will do nothing but blow dirt in. Erin, I'm so sorry!"

"You don't have to be. Let's change into our suits. We probably could wear our shorts and tee shirts over the suits. We haven't bought large beach towels yet so I guess we'll have to use the towels from here."

"Look" Wayne grabbed two colorful beach towels from the bed. "They supplied towels for us. I guess they are trying to give good service. Now we won't have to use sandy towels after our showers. I wonder if this morning's towels are still here?" Wayne walked into the bathroom. "Well, would you believe we do have fresh ones?"

"Well, we are getting nice surprises...so it won't be as bad as we had feared. Hey. Wayne, they put a table fan here in the bedroom. It isn't terribly big but it's better than nothing. You don't suppose it was here all the time and we just didn't notice? Would it be safe to turn it on now and leave it on...along with the ceiling fan...while we're gone?"

Wayne walked out of the bathroom and looked at the small fan. "Unless their wiring is below code it should be all right and that is exactly what we'll do. It might save us tonight. By the way, we haven't talked about where we should go to dinner." All I care about is good food and air conditioning but you might have a special place in mind. What are you hungry for?"

"You wouldn't want to return to Sizzler's?"

"I don't think Margie will be there for the breakfast as well as the dinner shifts. We can see her tomorrow for breakfast but wouldn't you like to find something else tonight? Maybe something Hawaiian?"

"It sounds wonderful but right now I'm trying to find my bathing suit!" Erin slowly took everything out of her suitcase, laying the clothes on the made bed. "Hey Wayne look, they made the bed for us. Gosh real room service. Towels and bed!" She laughed.

"Now if I can find my bathing suit." She slowly went through her clothes then checked her suitcase again.

"Oh good, here it is. I was beginning to think I'd forgotten it." She pulled a royal blue one piece suit out of a side pocket in her suitcase. She took thongs from her overnight bag and quickly stepped out of her shorts and underpants, stepped into her bathing suit, pulling it to her waist then pulling off her tee shirt and bra, dropping them to the bed, then quickly pulling it up and slipping her arms into the straps.

Wayne walked into the room while pulling off his tee shirt, shorts and white Y front undershorts. Naked he went to his suitcase and from the pocket in the top took out a pair of navy swim trunks and pulled them on. He stuck his feet into a pair of thongs and grabbed his towel for the beach.

Erin realized she was getting used to seeing Wayne so casually walking around the room naked. She was feeling more married each day and realized it didn't have to be sex to make her feel married. It was their natural unashamed attitude about their bodies. She had never seen her brothers without clothes and she had been careful to never let them see her; at least not since she was a very little girl and hadn't known any better. Now she was running around with Wayne naked with almost complete comfort. She would be doing this the rest of their lives and it felt good. She had nothing to hide from him. Remembering how quickly she had pulled up the bottom half and then the top half of her suit it seemed so silly after what they had had in bed and in the baths. They had washed each other's bodies and they had made love. Their wet bodies had clung together under the shower. Dressing and undressing in front of him was nothing and she would never be uncomfortable doing it again.

"Ready, Babe?"

"All ready. I'll get the lights here. It's amazing we should need lights during daylight in Hawaii but I'll leave the small fan on. I do believe that ceiling fan is helping." She held her arms up towards the ceiling. "I think this place will be okay for a week after all."

The drive to the beach was farther than Erin had expected. They drove out of Pearl City and up the coast. Wayne seemed to have a beach in mind as he passed a few Erin felt would be perfect. Wayne had said he had been to Waikiki to surf. Had he mentioned being here in Pearl City also? She couldn't remember. Wayne pulled off the road and parked at a wide white beach. A small hot dog stand was just off the road and it had beach umbrellas propped against its wall. A 'For Rent' sign was fastened to one of the umbrellas.

"Oh, Wayne, how perfect! Do you think we could have our lunch here and maybe rent an umbrella? It might help us to not get too burned this first day."

"Yeah, when I saw the hot dog stand I thought it might hit the spot for lunch. The beach and a hot dog. What could be better?" He smiled down at Erin. "Nothing and I agree we'd better have an umbrella. Why don't you go to the beach and pick out our spot and I'll rent a little shade for us. Then after we're settled we can get ourselves some food."

Erin popped out of the car and ran down to the beach, the sand covering her thongs like waves. She looked at the few couples and families already settled and chose a spot a little further down the beach. She dropped their towels and picking up one, opened it and spread it out on the hot sand, then spread the second next to it, leaving space to plant the umbrella. Wayne hurried across the sand carrying a multi-striped umbrella. He poked the pole deep into the sand as if he'd had lots of experience. He twisted it until it seemed secure and then opened it over the towels. Shade immediately covered them and Erin removed her shorts and tee shirt and dropped them onto the bottom of her towel. but left her thongs on for the walk through the sand back to the hot dog stand.

Wayne added his clothes to his towel and smiled down at her.

"Ready to eat, Babe?"

"More than ready. It seems hours since breakfast. Let's go see what they have. Do you find that the larger your breakfast is the hungrier you get for lunch? It doesn't make sense." She laughed.

The two grasped hands and ran back across the sand to the little red, white and blue stand. Hot dogs with the choice of mustard, mayonnaise, catsup, chopped onions. pickle relish, chopped tomatoes, salsa or sauerkraut were tempting. Frozen chocolate candy bars as well as ice cream bars for those who didn't mind getting messy. Bottled water and about every choice of carbonated drinks and packages of potato chips or peanuts were also listed on the chalk board. Erin looked at the menu and chose a hot dog with mustard and pickle relish. She felt these would be less messy.

"No onions, Babe?"

She looked at Wayne. "Are you going to have onions?"

"Sure, what's a hot dog without onions?" He laughed down at her.

"Well, if you are I am too." She looked up at the young man who was running the stand. "Would you put onions on mine too and I'll have some bottled water."

"I'll have a Coke and I think two packages of potato chips with mine." Wayne added.

The young man quickly took two hot dogs from the little grill and put them on buns and filled them with the condiments. He set them on paper plates with small bags of potato chips. He placed the two iced drinks on the counter next to the plates.

"That will be eight dollars...thirty cents." Wayne put a ten dollar bill on the counter, took the change and put it in a tiny pocket inside the top of his suit. He handed the two bottles to Erin and pulled some paper napkins out of a canister that sat on the counter. Then he picked up the two paper plates and turned to Erin. "Okay Babe, let's go."

They plodded back through the sand to their chosen site and Erin carefully lowered herself down and put the bottles on her towel and then reached up and took the plates from Wayne before he tried to sit down.

"Ohhhh, these look so good! I hadn't realized how hungry I am." She handed Wayne's plate to him, put hers on the towel and immediately picked up the hot dog and started to eat. "Heaven!" She grinned up at Wayne. "These are heaven! Have you ever tasted better?"

Wayne took a large bite and chewed slowly. "You're right, they are great. We just might need two."

Erin laughed. "I was thinking the same thing but do you think we should? We'll have dinner tonight and these cost us more than our breakfast. It's a good thing we saved as long as we did for this trip. It is expensive except, you know what hon.? I think the hot dogs at our beaches are the same price. There really is a mark up on this kind of simple food. Certainly these little stands don't have that much overhead. They have a good thing going, especially here. I wonder how successful they would be in San Diego?"

Wayne reached over and put his hand on Erin's free one. "Babe. this is our honeymoon and I don't want us to mention the cost with everything we do. We have money and if we don't we will just use my Visa card and take care of that bill after we get home. We are going to have fun. We are going to have a honeymoon we will remember all of our years together.

Agreed?"

Erin smiled. "Agreed! I won't mention costs again. I do have an idea though.

When we finish with this food let's take our swim before we work on our tans. I'm eager to get into that warm ocean. Then, after we are worn out from swimming we might want another hot dog. What do you think?"

"I think it sounds like a great idea. Let me know when you're ready to go in."

Wayne finished his hot dog and started on a bag of potato chips and then followed it with a large swallow of his coke.

"Darling I wouldn't mind if we did just this every day. This air is so great." She waved her arms in the air, waving her hot dog in circles above her head. "It's just as warm as our San Diego air can be but there is something different about the tropical feel."

Wayne turned over to his stomach and put his head down on the towel. "Yes, there isn't anything like this air...this does feel great and you're right, we should do it as often as we can."

Erin finished her hot dog, wiped bits of mustard and relish from her mouth, tucked the napkin under the towel so it wouldn't blow down the beach and took one more drink from her water, screwed the top back on and lay down next to Wayne. "There are so many things to see on this island. As wonderful as this is, wouldn't we feel badly if we missed them to roast in the sun every day?"

"I don't want you to get burned but you know we can come back and do the tourist things on another trip. We do have years of vacations ahead of us." Wayne spoke into his towel. "When I have thought of Hawaii I have thought of beaches. Lying on this glorious sand and soaking in the tropic air and sun. I know there are things to see and maybe we will change our mind when we get to Honolulu. I know there are things at Waikiki to see. Especially as we do have over three weeks more to fill. It's just when you are lying here like this...you never want to do anything else."

"Okay, we'll just wing it and plan each day as we get to it. In the meantime I'm enjoying this. Punch me if I go to sleep."

"I'm not going to go to sleep. I'm going into the water. Joining me?"

Wayne jumped up from his towel and gave Erin his hand. "Let's go!"

The water was like their bath. which surprised Erin. She hadn't expected it to be 'this' warm. "Oh, this is glorious," she shrieked as she jumped a wave. Then she pushed herself out past the breaking waves and lay on her back and floated, ignoring the lapping water that washed over her face. Wayne struggling to float next to her, knew he had never been happier

They played like children, splashing each other and tumbling in the water together. When the water began to feel cold, holding hands, they walked through the waves back to the hot sands and then ran, almost skipping, to avoid the burning. They jumped back onto the towels and fell into a heap together.

"Lu, is that you?"

Wayne froze for a minute and then slowly rolled onto his back and sat up.

"I'm afraid you have me mixed up with someone else. My name is Wayne and this is my wife Erin."

Erin looked up at the stranger standing above them. He was about Wayne's age only as blonde as she was. He looked like a typical surfer so she wondered why he was at this beach with its casual waves. How could he think he knew Wayne? She said nothing.

"I couldn't believe it when I saw you. It's been quite a while.

You left here when you were sixteen. Right?" He studied Wayne's face. You were about my only childhood friend. I've missed you, buddy."

"I'm sorry but you have made a mistake." Wayne looked at the sand.

"No I haven't. I would have known you anywhere. You look the same...just a little older." He smiled. "A little heavier and on you it looks good. You look like you've made a good life for yourself. Where are you living now?"

"I'm sorry but I am not this Lu you think I am."

The man stood looking down at the couple. He couldn't understand why his friend would deny who he was.

"I don't know why you don't recognize me and I don't understand why you deny knowing me but you are Lu Walters."

Erin looked at Wayne. He had paled and was looking more serious than she had ever seen before, almost frightened. This scared her but she just sat, listening. How could he be called Lu Walters? An old nickname? If this were true why wouldn't Wayne recognize his old friend?

"Did you know they found your mother?" Wayne looked up. "I'm sorry Lu, but she's dead. They found her dead about two weeks after you left. They figured someone broke in and killed her a few days after you were gone. They bound...I'm sorry but this could be rough on you and your wife but I think you should know what happened. They bound her legs, arms and mouth with duct tape and put her in a closet. She suffocated." He paused a moment then went on. "I have a theory about it Lu. When you were not seen around your place someone sensed you were gone and weren't a threat so broke in to see what they could get and your mother surprised him."

Erin put her hand over her mouth and looked at Wayne. He looked so strained she put a hand down on his. He looked into her eyes and then out to the sea...

He had murdered his mother. Bile rose in his throat and he swallowed quickly to keep from losing it on the sand. He put his hand over his mouth. My God, oh God! He hadn't expected her to die. Hadn't she taped him like that many times? She had fought him and he had worked quickly to get her secure enough to carry her into the closet just as she had done to him. Eventually his mother had returned to release him. His mother would be found, he had been so sure of that...he had never questioned...but she died. He had killed her! Then it hit him. He had killed twice. He felt faint and held tightly to Erin's hand but couldn't look at her again. He had to get away from here. Away from Tony and Pearl City but first he couldn't let on to Tony...he could never even suspect ...

"I didn't know." Wayne continued to sit quietly and then said without looking at his friend. "How you been, Tony? I didn't expect to see you on this beach." Erin looked at the two men, feeling confused and sick inside. What was happening? What had Wayne kept from her? She thought she knew this man she had married but now she was feeling a little frightened. His fingers were biting into hers.

Tony reached out to take Wayne's hand. "It's really good to see you man. Where did you go to?"

Wayne ignored the hand. "Mainland. I went to the mainland. California. You say my mother is dead? Do they know who killed her?" He swallowed hard again.

"No. I don't think the person meant to kill her...just accidentally cut off her air with the tape on her mouth. Then the closet was pretty air tight. Sorry Lu... but I thought you needed to know this. God, but I've missed you and I felt so sorry when they found her and you weren't here. They buried her. Lord...this is hard." He dug his toe into the sand. "I'm so sorry, friend but they buried her in a pauper's grave." Tony pulled his toe from the sand and then stood rocking from foot to foot in the heat but also from emotional discomfort. He couldn't look in Lu's eyes. "She had no one here to take care of her so....well, the State did. I don't know how much her estate had but your house is still there. Just empty. I think they kept hoping you would come home some day, find out what happened and claim the estate and house. I know you folks didn't have much, just as we didn't, but there is the house. I know it was rough on you and your mom after your dad left. I didn't see that much of you after that. You were my best friend, Lu. God, what a surprise this is. Guess you're surprised too...but what's with the new name?"

Wayne didn't look up but said almost under his breath. "If you were named for a girl would you want to live your entire life with a girl's name? Lucille? Would you want to be called Lucille? My folks always wanted a girl, especially my father. They didn't want me. I was treated like a girl." He didn't clarify his statement. "That's why I left as soon as I got old enough." He looked up at his old friend. "I don't hang around where I'm not wanted."

Erin sucked in her breath and clung even tighter to Wayne's hand to give him her support. She couldn't say anything in front of his friend but oh dear God, what had Wayne gone through when he was a child? It was no wonder he hadn't wanted to talk about his family when she'd asked. Her poor darling. She was responsible for their being here. The only place he wouldn't want to come to for their honeymoon... and Pearl City. Why had he agreed to it? He had lived here with his parents and it couldn't have been a happy childhood and now he had just found out that his mother was dead. Probably murdered. Would he carry this guilt for leaving her alone? She placed her second hand over his. He had to know this name change wouldn't make any difference to her. He had a house here. Here in Pearl City? Wayne held her hands so tightly it hurt but she said nothing. He had to be suffering so she just held on . Erin felt a little uncomfortable with this man looking down at her. Her hair, tied back in a pony tail was soaking wet and matted with sand. She wished for a wrap over her skimpy bathing suit but this was not the time to be concerned about her appearance. It was Wayne's obvious pain that worried her.

"Do you mind if I sit down for a minute? This sand is getting hot even with my thongs."

Wayne said nothing but made room for him on his towel. and moved a little closer to Erin. What was she thinking? He couldn't imagine and it terrified him. Losing her because of his lies was something he couldn't handle. How had Tony turned up at this beach on just this day? A few days more and they would have been further down the island and the chances of his running into anyone he knew would be almost impossible.

Tony Barcino, his only friend when he had needed one so badly. He had to say something to Erin.

"Hon., this is Tony Barcino. We were friends here at Pearl City. I grew up here and Tony was my only friend. Tony this is my wife, Erin." His eyes searched hers for understanding.

Erin couldn't let on to Tony she hadn't known of Wayne's name change. She released Wayne's hand and held out her right hand and smiled. "Hi, Tony, it's nice to meet you."

Tony reached past Wayne and took her hand. "Looks like Lu has done well by his self. How long you guys been married?"

Erin was embarrassed to admit they had just been married that week. "We haven't been married long but Wayne is my best friend too. I wanted a vacation in Hawaii and we chose Pearl City because it is less expensive than the rest of the island. Only, we have decided we aren't going to stay. In fact we were just about to leave here to go back to our hotel to pack."

Wayne looked at her with love and pride. He felt he could breath again. 'Tony. I don't have any property here. My folks never had enough money to buy a house. We always rented. That house was owned by an out-of-state owner. I haven't the remotest idea where and I could care less. I never want to see the place again. Anyone who broke in would be disappointed at what they found as there was never anything of value. Anything my mother brought into the marriage had been pawned long ago by my father."

Erin squeezed Wayne's hand. They would go back to their motel and pack immediately. They wouldn't stay here even one more night. It didn't matter where they went...what they had to pay. She just wanted to get Wayne away from these memories.

She wanted to build new, happier memories of his home island.

She stood, pulling Wayne with her. "It's been good meeting you, Tony but we do have to leave. I am glad to have met Wayne's friend. I'm sure you helped to make his life here happier." She smiled at him. "Now that's my job and I love it." She bent to pick up her towel.

Being kind, Tony used Lu's new name. "Wayne I've missed you and I'd like to keep in touch."

"Sure, of course, do that."

"Wayne. I need your address or phone number in California."

Wayne studied his friend for a moment. "Do you have a card? Give me your address. I'll get back to you after we get back to the mainland."

"Can't we get together again while you're here?"

Wayne almost exploded. "Tony, we are on our honeymoon. NO! We don't want to visit with anyone." He then tried to soften his tone to his old friend. "Sorry, it's just...all this has been such a surprise and shock."

"No. I'm sorry Lu...Wayne...I didn't realize. Of course you don't want a night out with an old friend. We can do that another time. Maybe I'll get to California someday.

I'm a shoe salesman in Honolulu so the money isn't great but I'll try to make it. Where did you say you live in California?"

"I guess I didn't. San Diego. We live in San Diego but we will be moving as soon as we get back. We're needing to find a larger place so I don't have an address to give you. I guess you don't have a card in your swim suit. We'll be listed after we get settled and besides, I remember your address. I'll get in touch with you. It might be easier."

Tony stood and embraced his old friend. "Wayne, we only had each other all those years but now it looks as if you have all the support you need." He smiled at Erin.... "Congratulations, guy. I envy you."

"You're not married yet?"

"Who would want a scruff like me? I work to get by and then I surf. That's still my big love." He smiled again.

Wayne relaxed a little. "Well, we do have some big waves in San Diego so maybe sometime you can get there."

"What do you do? I mean for your living?"

"I'm a sales rep for auto parts. California is my territory, so you see, I'm gone much of the time."

"Auto parts. I might have known. Your father did like to putter with old cars. I remember you always had lots of old cars in your yard. You were good. I'll bet you could build a car from the ground up if you wanted to."

Wayne smiled. "Probably could, but we really have to go now." He held out his hand this time. "It's been good seeing you and thanks, thanks for telling me about my mother."

"I can tell you where she was buried. You might want to take a run by and see it."

Wayne looked down at the ground. "I don't think so but thanks." He looked up at his old friend. "This is supposed to be a happy time for us. I can see the grave another time...you understand."

"Sure, sure thing." Tony took Wayne's hand again and shook it firmly then reached over and held his hand out to Erin. She promptly took it and gave it a firm shake.

"I'm glad you recognized Wayne. Wasn't it something that out of all of the beaches along here and of all the days you both wound up here at the same time. I believe things are meant to happen and this was one of them. Unfortunately, you had the bad news of Wayne's mother but I will see that we do get back here. He will want to see her grave. Maybe we can even move her. It's just that right now...well...it's a special time for us and this has all been quite a shock for him, for us....you understand, I'm sure."

"Sure, I understand and I think you're quite a girl. Wayne you're a lucky guy. Hope I can get as lucky someday."

Wayne smiled. Lucky, if he only knew. God, if he only knew! Wayne casually. picked up his towel, shook out the sand, folded it and handed it to Erin. They pulled on their shorts and Wayne draped the tee shirts over his arm as they slipped into their thongs.

"Oh, Wayne. I almost forgot...I saw your dad yesterday."

Wayne did a double take and then just stood seemingly frozen for a few minutes and then spoke in a forced voice. "Where?"

"Here in Pearl City. Guess he's working here now. He didn't recognize me and I didn't say anything to him. Why should I?

He never paid attention to me when we were kids and he left you and your mom. I always felt you never cared that much for him. I just thought you might want to know he is still alive and here."

"Thanks. Yeah, I'm glad to know he's here." he tried to smile. "Now I can be careful to avoid him. Well, we gotta go. Ready Erin?"

"Ready, let's go." She checked their belongings and turned back to Wayne's friend and smiled as she offered her hand again. "It was a nice surprise to meet you Tony. We would like to have you come for a visit." With that comment she turned and headed for the car, Wayne just behind her. They didn't look back again but climbed into the hot car and quickly pulled out of the parking spot and headed back to Pearl City and their Hawaiian palace....

The ride back was quiet. Wayne had his thoughts and Erin knew this wasn't the time to ask questions. She would learn the answers when it was the right time for him. Wayne parked in front of their 'cottage.' Erin carried the towels and shirts into the living room and plopped them down on the worn brown couch, not caring about the wet and sand. The fan in the ceiling was still shirring, moving the hot air. The small fan purred with a slight click.

"I'm going to see the manager and tell him we have just had bad news and we have to leave right away."

"You won't be telling him anything but the truth. I'll start packing. I know you don't want to take any chance of running into your father. I could tell darling, that you were uncomfortable seeing your old friend and I know from what little was said that you don't want to take any chances of seeing your father. We'll just leave here and drive to Honolulu and find a place to stay for the rest of the week."

Wayne looked at his wife. "I'm sure you have lots of questions you want answered and I wouldn't blame you."

"Darling, I have no questions. When you want to tell me more about your past you can and I'll be glad to listen but I am not going to pry. Obviously it wasn't a happy childhood or you would have told me more before now. You hadn't even told me you had lived near Pearl City and now I feel guilty because I talked you into an Hawaiian honeymoon. You never said a word. You just went along with the idea. I will always be sorry you did, especially our staying in Pearl City. Anyplace but here would have been safer for you." Tears came to her eyes.

Wayne held her close and then lifted the little face with his hands and looked into her blue eyes. Today they seemed as blue as the ocean they had just left. "Erin, honey, you must never, never feel guilty about our coming here. I think I agreed because I was having a sense of being drawn here, after all these years. It must have been right that I come or I wouldn't have met Tony again. I wouldn't have found out what happened to my mother and that my dad is here in town. You see? I was guided and you were a part of it. But...right now I need a long, hot shower. I feel dirty." He thought back to Aunt Mary and now his mother. "You'll never know how dirty I feel!" He laid his head on her wet, sandy hair and just held her closer for a moment. "Then I'll go to the office and tell them we are leaving. On second thought I'd like you in that long hot shower with me." He said into her hair and then looked into her eyes. She answered by slipping out of her shorts and bathing suit there in the living room and walked naked to the bathroom. Wayne followed..

Chapter 12

The drive to Honolulu was quiet. Wayne had no trouble from the motel manager when told there had been a tragedy in the family and they had to leave immediately. He was billed for the short stay and Pearl City would soon be behind them.

Erin watched Wayne's face as he drove. It was obvious he was trying to work many things out in his mind. Erin felt he had more than hearing about his mother's death on his mind or possibly that his father was in Pearl City. She wanted to question him about his past but decided to just wait. They had vowed to never keep secrets but this was more than just a secret.

"Erin, I need to talk with you. I need to tell you everything about my childhood. I haven't shared it with anyone else but I need to tell you but would you mind if I wait until we get settled tonight? I don't want to talk about it while I'm driving."

"Wayne, you don't have to ever tell me. I'll love you no matter what your name is. Your past is your past. It's our future that I am looking forward to."

Wayne lifted his right hand off the wheel for a moment and put it on Erin's left leg. He said nothing more.

In a few minutes he pulled the car in front of the Hale Pua Nui at 228 Beach Walk. "Wayne, this is where we are coming next week. Do you think they will have room for us now?"

"Darling. there is only one way to find out. The way this day has gone I wouldn't be surprised at anything. You might as well wait here. I'll be right out, hopefully to get you."

Erin sat in the car and tried to get her bearings. They had said the beach was a five minute walk from here but she wasn't sure which direction. Palm trees, shrubs and flowers were all around. Obviously this was an older neighborhood but it was clean, neat and tropical with the plantings. She loved all of it. It was so Hawaii was all she could think.

Wayne's face was at the car window. "We're in luck. A couple left this morning and they have just finished cleaning that unit. Best yet, it can be our unit the rest of the month and we get the rest of this week at a discount."

Wayne opened the back doors and took out their suitcases. He would get the wet. sandy towels from the trunk after they had gotten settled in. They needed to have more shaking and a good drying if they were to use them on the beach tomorrow. They would need to return them to the 'palace' in Pearl City after they'd been laundered. A good reason to purchase their own beach towels they could somehow squeeze into their suitcases.

"Oh, Wayne, twin beds." She pretended horror. "Which one shall we sleep in?" She said laughing.

Wayne put the two suitcases down on the floor and carefully checked out the situation. "Ok. it looks as if we have air conditioning after all and we have two ceiling fans so we should stay cool enough for cuddling. How about the bed closest to the windows? Hey, check out that view Erin. Being on a third floor instead of the first has it's advantages. This is great." He turned to Erin who was looking at the kitchenette. "Is there a problem?"

Erin looked up smiling. "Oh, Wayne. I'm so glad we came here. This is so cute. Look how compact all of it is. I don't think I will do any gourmet meals here but we certainly can survive. We do want to eat a few meals out anyway, right?" She opened some cupboards and found four of everything. Dishes, glassware, silverware, place mats for the small table as well as basic pots and pans. A coffee maker stood on the small counter. A little refrigerator had two tiny ice cube trays.

"I wonder how far shopping is? We will want to pick up groceries tomorrow now that we know how much room we have for storage. We'll just shop for a few days at a time. Oh Wayne, this is going to be so much fun. I love it. This is our home for almost a month and we can put the past two days behind us." Wayne's face had reflected her joy but then turned sober again.

"Erin, can we sit on the couch and talk?"

"Yes, of course...but...are you sure you don't want to unpack our suitcases, eat and maybe even get ready for the night before we talk?"

"We haven't had dinner yet so maybe you're right. We should unpack and then find a place to eat...then we can talk when our emotions aren't on empty stomachs." He went to Erin and held her close...her face pressed next to his chest. He didn't kiss her at this time. He wanted to be very sure of what her emotions really were.. what her thoughts of this afternoon were before he pressed his luck. He knew what she had been saying but she hadn't heard the whole story. Maybe he had only until after their meal to have her total love and support. The thought terrified him again and he just held her more tightly. Feeling her little body next to his...would he have this tonight? Oh, God, he was so scared. She loved him, he was sure of that but how strong was that love? Why did he often doubt? Why was he so frequently afraid of losing her? Was it because he had never been loved before? Did his past make him unworthy of being loved? It wasn't his fault...he'd been just a boy, a little boy. Wayne looked around their honeymoon room and took a deep breath. Would the filth of his past be too much for her? God! Would he ever feel clean? Killing Aunt Mary had been bad but this...sweat was building on his forehead.

He was the first to pull away. Without saying a word they

each took a suitcase and opening them on the floor started unpacking. A clothes closet with a long single rod and dozens of plastic hangers and a blonde rattan dresser with six drawers handled the summer clothes easily. Their things were now side by side for the first time. In Pearl City they had lived out of their suitcases.

Erin smiled at Wayne as he stood next to her. "It looks right, doesn't it?"

"Yes sweetheart, it looks very right." He struggled to sound calm.

"Do you think we need to change for supper?"

"No, I think for tonight we can find a fast food place for a quick meal so we don't have to change. While we are out we can find a grocery store and pick up a few things."

"Wayne, would you like it if we bought groceries and came back here to fix our first meal?"

"No, I see they have dish soap and towels but you've had a full day too and I think we can just eat simply tonight and tomorrow we can start our month here. You can play housewife...tomorrow." After hearing what he had to tell her...would she stay and how much of the past should he...would he have to tell her? There was certainly one part he wouldn't tell her. He would never tell anyone. Not even Erin could live with him if she knew the whole truth.

Erin picked up her little purse and took Wayne's hand." Cum mon. Let's find that quick place to eat. We can fill our stomachs and then get back here to have our talk and then loving. Darling, after what you learned today all I want to do is love you. That's all I really want! Except that my stomach disagrees with me, I don't want dinner." She gave him a quick kiss and pulled at her husband. Wayne followed, his emotions tearing at him.

McDonalds. Not exactly Hawaiian food but enough to fill the hollows in their middles. Hamburgers with sliced pineapple. Okay, that could be Hawaiian, at least different. A salad bar. Erin suddenly realized how good fresh greens would taste but Wayne chose a double hamburger without onions and a chocolate milkshake. Erin took machine made iced tea. They settled down in a booth and found they didn't have much to talk about. Neither wanted to rehash the day They talked about their luck at getting into the Hale Pua Nui at this time and how perfect it was for them.

Erin had heard of a wonderful place full of shops and stalls for shopping and Wayne assured her there were many of them but she was probably thinking of the International Market Place. Wayne was sure they would both end up with at least one Hawaiian shirt. He hadn't worn the 'tourist' type when growing up in Hawaii and he was going to avoid it now if he could. There would be good looking patterns that didn't shriek "Hawaii tourist" and would feel comfortable in San Diego. He would try to guide Erin to these, if she was still with him.

Wayne drove the car out of the McDonald's parking lot and headed back to Beach Walk. He felt a little better except for the knot in his middle. The food hadn't relaxed that. Wayne didn't want to talk about anything except how much he loved Erin. Except for a terrible fear around his heart it was all he could feel. Would she want to hear it later?

"Erin, you know you are my life. You have been since I first saw you. I never heard love expressed when I was growing up. When I was born I know my parents didn't want me...they wanted a daughter so I was named a girl's name and treated like a girl. I was a disappointment to them but I fear I am or will be a disappointment to you and this tears me apart. I feel as if I have a tight band around my heart. I didn't love my parents...I feared them most of the time. I tolerated being with them until I was old enough to leave." Erin started to speak but he put his hand on her lips. "Let me finish while I can.

I worked hard to earn a living and I worked my way up from a mechanic to a salesman. I think I have told you that. I wasn't happy...I was content as I was away from my parents. Then I met you. You know how I feel about you. I love you completely and you will be the only woman I will ever love but I want you to know that after our talk tonight I don't want you to feel obligated to stay with me. I couldn't stand that. You are free to go any time you need to. If you can no longer love me....well, I will understand." Erin took a breath to speak but Wayne shook his head. "Please, let me say what I need to say.

You have already given me more in my life than I have ever had and if this is it I thank you with all my heart. You will always have it, no matter where I am." Tears welled up in Wayne's eyes. "Erin, I can't finish here Let's not talk anymore until we are back 'home.'"

Erin sat quietly...watching Wayne's face. What could possibly kill her love for him? What kind of a horrible past was he going to tell her? Nothing would change the way she felt about him. Needing to touch him she reached over and put her hand on his right thigh. She needed some kind of closeness. She was scared. Scared for her Wayne, for their love.

Wayne walked into the third floor unit just ahead of her and turned the lights on. Erin headed for the white rattan couch. The cushions looked new and were white background with large beige, brown and yellow floral prints. Not a California print but it fit the lush tropical environment she saw everywhere.

Wayne sat down across from her although she would rather have had him next to her where she could touch him, hold his hand...just give him her support. Her insides began to churn, maybe eating before their talk hadn't been a very good idea. She had a real fear of what was to come.

Wayne sat looking at his hands in his lap...afraid to look at Erin. "I guess my earliest days were as normal as most families. I don't remember my parents expressing affection. I think children are aware of love and affection early. 'IT' began when I was just four years old. My mother took me into the bathroom and put me in a warm tub and bathed me all over. Everyplace. She then towel dried all of my parts...especially...and put little girl white under pants on me. They had a narrow band of white lace around the leg openings and on the waist." Erin started to speak but Wayne held up his hand. "She then slipped a girls white slip over my head and then a cotton dress of a small rosebud print. She carefully brushed my hair which they kept cut to just above my shoulders." Wayne took a deep breath before he went on." My mother then took me by the hand and led me to their bedroom. My father was already sitting on the edge of the bed and held his arms out to me."

Wayne breathed hard for a few minutes and Erin was tempted to go to him but he sensed her slight movement and put his hand up again, took a deep breath and went on. "My father pulled me to him and reaching up he pulled the dress over my head and carefully laid it next to him on the bed, then the slip. Then....he pulled the panties down around my ankles. I stood in front of him naked. He kissed me on the neck and then moved his kisses to all over my body. I was scared and uncomfortable but too afraid to try to move away.

Then my father. my father.... bent me over the edge of the bed with my face down and he put his tongue in my crack and moved it all around getting it wet. Then he put his finger or fingers up inside me. He would move them back and forth and wider apart...stretching the opening. It was so painful but I

115

couldn't move. I didn't dare. Then he took his fingers out and...then...then he put me up on the bed on my hands and knees with my head down on the bed. My bum was facing him and then something hard was pounding...pushing at my bottom and then....it suddenly went in. I screamed into the quilt but he kept pushing... in and out...making strange sounds until he would moan or cry out and then he pulled it out. I didn't know for a long time what it was he put inside of me. I just knew the pain was terrible. If I ever tried to protest I got a hard slap on the side of my head.

Erin put her hand over her mouth. Tears rolled down her cheeks but she said nothing.

"I can remember getting off of the bed crying and turning around...I saw my mother standing in the bedroom doorway watching. She had watched this terrible thing that my father had done to me. She took me by the hand...back to the barely warm...used bathwater and would bath me. She would wash off blood and something else and always told me how much I had pleased my father and so I had also pleased her.

The next day...at the same time...the ritual was repeated. It was repeated every day until I was twelve when I suddenly realized I was taller than my father and I was able to say. "Never Again!" Two days later my father left our house and never returned. "

"Oh darling..."

"No. Please Erin, let me finish. I have to finish.

Because my father left us my mother punished me. She would beat me for the slightest infraction. Even a look would bring on a belt beating. My father's belt.

She was always careful to beat me where it didn't show. Never on my arms or legs, just the soft parts of my body. I wasn't allowed to have friends or to leave the house without her permission. When I did she would tape my ankles and wrists together when I was asleep. Then she would roll me off the bed and into the closet where she would lock me in until she felt like letting me out or...when she came back from some errand. If she left for a long time she put duct tape over my mouth. I really got it the time she discovered that Tony and I had taken a bus to Waikiki for a day. I was in the closet for three days and nights. I had to soil myself and I had no food or water. She hadn't known I had Tony as a friend but I never told him what was going on in our house. I think sixth grade was the last time I went to school. It was about the time my father left. Before then...except for his ritual with me he would teach me about repairing cars. He was very good and could have built a car completely alone.

He did give me a training which has made it possible for the job I have now. I guess I have to thank him for that. I thank him for nothing more." He looked at Erin. Tears were running down her face as she quietly sobbed. Fear pulled at his stomach.

Seeing him look at her she felt free to speak but she wasn't sure she could speak. She was so horrified, so sickened by what he had told her.

"I did this to you, Wayne. I'm so sorry, so terribly sorry. I was responsible for having all of these memories come back. If I hadn't asked for a Hawaiian honeymoon this wouldn't have happened. Certainly you wouldn't have seen your old friend again. You wouldn't have learned about your mother and you wouldn't have learned that your father is still on the island. I'm sure, even though we have moved away from Pearl City you will be constantly looking over your shoulder...afraid you will see him. Oh darling, I have done this to you." Fresh tears covered her face.

"No. Oh, no Erin. It wasn't your fault. There has hardly been a day in my life that I haven't remembered...but meeting you and having your love...having you in my life has given me happiness I never had before. Babe, you have been my salvation." He stood and went to her. Their arms went around each other and Wayne covered her tears with kisses.

"Oh, Wayne," she sobbed into his chest. "Those sick, sick monstrous people. How could they treat a baby that way? That is just what you were...a baby. Oh, I hate them. I hate them!" She looked up into eyes that were filled with pain.

"She deserves to be in a pauper's grave. Forgive me for saying that but she is just where she should be. Alone and unknown and most of all, unloved. She was your mother and for that I thank her as she gave me you but I will never honor her."

Wayne's tears blended with hers as he kissed her with slow, warm kisses, trying to ease her pain and fury, their pain and fury. He picked her up in his arms and carried her to bed.

Wayne had been right. The single bed nearest the windows had been just the right size, especially for that night. They had cuddled, holding each other close, turning together and when awake, kissing. It wasn't until the morning sun shone in their windows they made love. It was more than sex. It was a passionate struggle to heal, support for each other that left them both exhausted.

Wayne had told Erin all he dared and they didn't discuss last night's subject until they were about to leave the bed for their showers.

"Wayne, I did a little thinking last night and suddenly came up with a possible answer to what happened to your mother. Like who killed her."

Wayne looked at the little face so close to his. "What do you mean? Who do you think did it?"

"Your father"

Wayne hardly dared to move. When he felt composed he said, "Why do you think my father had anything to do with it?"

"I think it's obvious, darling." She scooted back to the edge of the bed so she could look at his face better, she was feeling quite proud of herself. "Your father left your mother and you for years. Well, when he somehow learned you had left he came back, who knows for what? He might have wanted to reconcile or maybe he just wanted to come back for some of his belongings, feeling he had a better chance when you were no longer around. Maybe he needed his tools but just hadn't dared to get them before. Your mother probably rejected him or threatened him. You know, .for what he had done to you, he never could have proved she had watched and had enjoyed it. They didn't have you as a witness. They had no idea where you were. I think we should go to the police or a lawyer...someone. They could find your father and throw the book at him."

Wayne had to laugh at her last quote, then became serious. "Babe, you could have something there but you know what? I don't really want my past brought out in the open even if it meant having my father punished for it. I don't want it on TV or in the newspapers. It would always follow us. I don't want that for us. Can't we just try to forget it? Can't we just go on with our lives as we have planned? I have always hoped my father's conscience was punishing him. The only thing I have feared was that he might have gone on and found another young child to abuse as he did me. That haunts me."

"Darling, that is why I felt he should be caught...so he could be stopped."

"I know, honey but it would be punishment for us if I had to face him or even if my name came out in the news."

"How would they find you? You have used the name Wayne ever since you left Hawaii. This is the first time you have returned and you're still using Wayne."

"Social Security number. Tax numbers. There are many ways I could be found if someone wanted me for something. I love you for thinking about what could help me but publicity wouldn't do it. I would rather stay… 'hidden'…if that's all right with you."

"Of course it's okay with me. I just thought it was obvious that your father did it.

His being in Pearl City shows he thinks he doesn't have anything to be afraid of. You aren't going to tell on him and your mother can't. He probably took everything from the house he wanted after he stashed your mother in the closet. I find it interesting that he taped her and put her in the closet…just what she did to you. He couldn't have known what she had done, could he? Wayne, some of those times your mother went out and left you bound, could she have been meeting your father?"

"My God, I never thought of that. I never would have dreamed she would do that but she did love him. It had to have been a sick love but I always knew she loved him more than she did me. But on the other side of that…when I pleased him, he left her alone sexually and that is possibly why she allowed it." Wayne tried to laugh. "I was afraid I'd lose you when I told you about my past and here you are not only supporting me again but coming up with possible solutions. What kind of television do you watch? Your thinking is wonderful but hardly the you I know…you are adorable and amazing and my admiration for you grows every day. Especially these last two days."

They lay on the bed wrapped in damp towels, their arms around each other. The sun was high above the trees when they awakened "What do you suppose a Hawaiian breakfast would be?" Erin asked as she blew lightly into Wayne's ear. He laughed. "I think it's time we find out. Afterwards we can see what mischief you can get into in the shops. I have already found out what mischief you can get into here. I'm not really sure how much more I can handle but I'm willing to try." He pulled her tight again and the towel fell from her body.

He sat on the edge of the bed watching her brush her beautiful hair. This would be something he would never tire of seeing but he had to be serious for a moment. "Babe, do you know what terrified me most yesterday?"

She turned to look at him, the brush held in her lap. "What?"

"The possibility of losing you."

"Losing me? How could that be? How could I not love you more for the pain your parents put you through? How could I not want to protect you from any other pain and to give you the love you never had before?"

"I don't think there are many women who would stick around with a man who had my past." Wayne sat just looking at Erin until the silence became uncomfortable. "Erin, you won't believe how dirty I feel. I haven't felt clean since I was four years old."

"But darling, you shower several times a day. You always wear clean clothes...how could you not feel clean?"

"It's a different dirt. It's inside and can't be reached with showers or clean clothes. God knows I've tried!" He put his hands over his face to cover his pain.

Erin moved close to him again. Tears welled in her eyes. "Can't I help you some way? Oh darling, I can't stand to see you hurting this much."

"Love me, Erin. I wish you could always love me...but I don't think it will be possible. It will be too much to ask."

"How can you say that? I'll always love you unconditionally! You are my life and always will be...My gosh, you saw a different side of me yesterday. I could have killed your mother and father because of what they did to you. I had thought I'd have your mother's body moved to a good grave but now…no way! She stays where she is and I'm glad. I'd fight to my death for you…I know I sound dramatic…like a cat, fighting for her kitten or …a mother fighting for her child. Wayne, I love you that much and I always will. No! Matter! What! Do you hear me darling? I will always love you…No! Matter! What is in your past…your past is your **past**!…I am your future!"

Wayne could do nothing but hold his wife. Yes, she had shown a fighting side yesterday but how much would she have fought for him if she knew he had not only killed his mother but her aunt. The irony was that Erin decided his father had killed his mother and it had fit…wouldn't it be something if his father was accused of murder. He almost felt sorry for him. Could he live with that? Would he have to confess what he had done? An accidental killing of a woman who had abused him. Still murder he was sure. Then there was Aunt Mary. Another accident, at least not intentional, but a murder in the eyes of the law and, he was sure, Erin.

"Wayne…Wayne…darling, are you okay?"

He couldn't share his thoughts. They had promised no secrets but these…

"Darling you seemed so far away…I think it's time we check out breakfast and the shops. I want you to always share your feelings, even your pain, with me but I think we have had enough for the last two days. Let's have fun today. Fun and love." Erin took his face in her hands. "You have earned the right to have both and I am going to spend my life seeing that you have both…" She kissed him gently. "Now, let's go eat and shop. I feel like going Hawaiian."

Chapter 13

"You look like a real Wahine." Erin looked at him questionably. "Wahine is Hawaiian for beautiful woman. Your Holoku is beautiful on you and the coral necklace is perfect with it."

"I was looking for shirts for both of us, not just a dress and necklace for me. They are beautiful though." She grinned at him as she held out her skirt. "This Holoku is slimmer than the usual muumuu. I think I would have drowned in the ones we saw. This is better on my flat figure." She twirled around the room in front of Wayne.

"Erin Walters have you ever looked at the high paid models? They are tall and slim. Very slim and flatter than you are. Yet, they are the envy of most women in the world. The only difference between you and them is that you, my darling, are shorter and I like you that way. I love everything about you so I don't want to hear anymore complaints about your figure. That dress is perfect for you and now we just have to find a special place to show you off when we go out to dinner tonight. I have never been here before…as an adult…so we will have to check things out together. Let's look in the drawers here in the kitchen. Maybe there will be brochures for places to dine out." Wayne opened three drawers and found only kitchen tools so he went to a small table next to the couch. "Bingo, here they are."

They sat together and poured over the "Where to Go and What to Do and Where to Eat" brochures. Hamburger Mary's, The New Tokyo Restaurant, Pizzeria Uno, Moose McGillycuddy's."

"What is that? It sounds interesting."

Wayne opened the folder. "Well, it serves from breakfast

through dinner. It closes at 10:00 p.m.. It's popular with the college crowds and has burgers, sandwiches, Mexican food, salads, Pupus and drinks at moderate prices."

"Pupus? What are they?"

"I think it's an appetizer served in a shell but I might be wrong. Remember, I'm new at this too. What about the rest of the food? There is nightly music and dancing.. That might be fun but are you in the mood for hamburger… sandwich… Mexican food or a salad bar?"

"Well, we had a hot dog for lunch yesterday so I think any of these would be okay. Mexican food isn't exactly Hawaiian but I may be dressed for dancing so what do you think?"

"I've never danced but if it gives me another chance to hold you in my arms I'm game."

"What else is there?"

"This one isn't real close but I think I could find it. Ono Hawaiian Food on Kapahulu Ave. It says we may have to wait in line but if we leave now, or after I shower,…we will be a little early for their dinner so the wait shouldn't be too long. They are open until 7:00pm. What do you think Erin?"

"That sounds like fun. A real Hawaiian dinner. Any wait will be worth it. I don't think we're in a rush, are we?"

"Okay. Ono's it is. I'll clean up. Would my cream slacks and a white dress shirt open at the neck meet your approval?"

"I'd go with you the way you are but if you think you want to change, your idea sounds fine. This should be fun and a very different experience but tomorrow we eat in.

Well maybe…if we are out at lunch time we can eat lunch out but breakfast and dinner I cook. I have to start being domestic sometime."

"You shouldn't have to do that on your honeymoon but if you don't mind, it might be nice just being alone here together.

I can't get over how scared I was last night. I still can't believe you are sticking with me. I'm still afraid of losing you." He folded his arms across his middle. The knot was still there.

"Lose me? Didn't we pledge for better and for worse until death do us part? What do you think you did that was awful enough for me to leave you? To break my vow of eternal love for you? Darling, you were the victim. Do you punish the victim? I will spend my life trying to undo the pain you suffered all of those years. If anyone was wrong about this trip it was me. I brought us here."

Wayne moved to Erin. "Darling. we promised we wouldn't discuss that again. As I said, it seemed to be something that needed to happen and I thank you for making it happen. I saw my old friend again and I have often wondered about him. My mother is dead and buried and my father is still alive and working. Probably in Pearl City. I will avoid that area now that I know. That is that! I don't have to wonder about these three again. They were a part of my past life but have no part of my life now or my future. You are my life now and you have given me a family and real friends so I will be happy…I am happy…I have never been happier."

"Wayne…may I say something else?"

He laughed and it felt good as it wasn't what he had expected this morning." "Well, I'd be careful if I were you."

Erin looked up at her husband to see his eyes. Was he serious or kidding her. His dark brown eyes were smiling.

"Okay, why don't I make an anonymous call to the police and tell them that your father, what ever his name is, is working in Pearl City and that they should look into where he was at the time your mother was bound and put in that closet. Say it is thought he had returned to the home after his son had left and confronted his wife. There could have been a fight and he could have put her in the closet to die." She watched his eyes. They were now dark and quiet. "Oh Wayne, you don't like the idea? How would anyone know it came from us? He needs to be punished even if your mother was as evil as he was. He needs to pay for what he did to you."

Wayne took her shoulders and led her to the couch where he sat her down and then sat next to her…looking into her face. "My precious darling. NO! I don't want any publicity here about this. It is bound to get stateside and eventually it would come around to us. Please forget it. Leave it alone. No more ideas. No more talk. Agreed?"

Tears came to Erin's eyes. This was the first time in all of the months they had known each other that Wayne had disciplined her and it hurt. She had disappointed him and it hurt. She had wanted so much to help to put his terrible father in jail for the rest of his life so as to protect any other child he might be hurting. The very thought of what he had done sickened her and it was hard to understand why Wayne didn't want him caught. But he had said no, so she had to honor his wishes as hard as it would be.

He held her close and then kissed her wet eyelids. "I'm sorry. Babe but you won't let go. I can understand your feelings about this but I don't want publicity that will touch our lives. I had to tell you about my past and I know yesterday brought up many questions for you but now I'm sorry I told you. It mustn't spoil our honeymoon. This month is ours. It is for now and something we can enjoy remembering in the future.

There is a higher power who will take care of my father. Hopefully he now is too old to abuse other children so I am not going to let myself think about him. For me he is dead.

My mother is dead but I have you. I have told you I have no life without you sooooooo, let's dry your eyes, kiss and make up and then go find Kapahulu Avenue."

Erin put her arms up around Wayne's neck and kissed his face and then his lips. "As long as you still love me after our disagreements, I'll be okay. I never meant to hurt you and I'll try to never do it again."

"You didn't hurt me. You were hurting for me and wanted to fix it. You just couldn't see that it could hurt us but I think you do now so let's forget about it and go have our dinner."

Chapter 14

"This is heaven. Absolute heaven. Waikiki Beach was fun but this, this is heaven! Waimea Bay. I could stay here forever. We have two more days, can we spend them here?"

Wayne rolled over onto his stomach so he could look at Erin. "This is your favorite spot after everything we have done? We have been pretty busy especially after our decision to just relax at the beaches. I've seen more of Waikiki this month than I did the entire sixteen years I lived on Oahu."

"Wayne," she said as she ran her finger down the length of his nose to his lips. "You hardly had a normal life...it certainly didn't include sightseeing. Besides, don't you think tourists usually see more of a country than residents do? This is going to push me to explore San Diego more. I have always taken things for granted and I've had a 'tomorrow' attitude. Does that sound like fun? Should we do that after we get back?"

Wayne was holding her index finger in his mouth so he just smiled and nodded his head.

"I will relive this month for the rest of my life. The Royal Hawaiian Hotel lunch was one of my favorite's. The Kapiolani Park. Our Balboa Park is similar with the Zoo but the Kodak Hula Show was fun and the Royal Hawaiian Band concert was great. There is so much to see and do but this...this is my favorite." Erin lay on her back and stretched out her arms to the sun. "You would think I never got sun at home but this air, so different and that warm water is pure heaven. She rolled back onto her stomach and looked at Wayne. "Feel like another dip?"

"Sure but just be careful of the coral. I'd never known about these beach shoes that protect your feet from getting cut when

I lived in Pearl City. Guess they are a fairly new idea." He held his feet up to admire the beach shoes they had been advised to buy. "Not that I went to the beach that often....but we're forgetting that story." He rolled over onto his stomach, got on his knees and stood looking down at his bride.

"You look like a native. You tan so evenly and you haven't burned once. I was afraid your being a blonde might give you trouble with the sun. You look beautiful!" He stood looking at her, admiring his bride who lay on her back with her arm outstretched. her hand waving to him…asking for a help up. Wayne laughed and then taking her hand he gently pulled her to her feet and into his arms. He didn't kiss her. not here on the beach. Holding hands they walked from the beach to float again in the warm salt water.

Erin had taken a lone shower so she could wash her long hair. It was so full of salt water and sand she'd had a hard time removing her pony tail clip. The hairs were tangled in every direction and she briefly thought she was going to have to cut it. She held it under the shower, wetting the hair until the tangles loosened. Then she poured shampoo into her hand and rubbed the lather through her hair. She thought of the wonderful day and the two more they had ahead of them. She'd had fun cooking meals, finding the challenge of this miniature kitchen. Tonight they would have a crab salad and freshly baked bread. The Luau they'd attended last night had been fun but obviously a tourist thing. Someday she would like to attend one with fewer people. The crowd had made it seem so commercial. fun but commercial. People had been dressed in every combination of clothes. Some had gone way out with colorful Hawaiian Muu-Muu's and wild floral shirts. She had worn her new Hawaiian dress and had felt comfortable although a little like a tourist. They hadn't found shirts they felt would be comfortable in San Diego so passed on that purchase. Actually they had spent little time or money shopping for 'things.' Wayne had found a beautiful hand carved wooden bowl they could use for fruit on her little breakfast table. Tomorrow they would beach it again but Wayne had suggested they try the well known Hanauma Bay beach and see the Toilet Bowl. She laughed at the name so was curious to see if it was well named. The next day would be their last and now it didn't seem possible they had spent a whole month in this glorious state.

Erin gave her hair a final rinse under the shower head and then twisted her hair to get the excess water out. She grabbed the towel at the end of the tub and started drying first her hair and then her body. When she was no longer dripping she stepped out of the tub and wrapped the damp towel around herself and opening the door, walked quietly into the living area. Wayne was talking on the phone and she stopped when she heard his conversation.

"I think you will find Irvine Walters working in Pearl City. He was seen there this month. No…I didn't see him…I was told by an old friend that he is there." There was a pause as he seemed to be listening. "Look, as I said, I am his son but I was in the states when my mother died. I feel there is a very good chance that my father returned when he found I was no longer living with my mother. He must have confronted her and knowing their past relationship I wouldn't have been surprised if it became violent. He was that kind of a person, I'm sorry but I am leaving for the mainland. You can do what you want with this information. I really am not that interested in what happens to him. I haven't seen him since I was twelve. This is the first time I have been back to Hawaii since I was sixteen. I wasn't going to call you about my suspicions until I was told my father is back in Pearl City. I am sure he feels very safe with my mother gone and my whereabouts unknown. He may be innocent but I am concerned of other crimes he might be involved in. I have no intention or desire of becoming involved. Twelve years with him were enough. I put him in your lap." Oh, God, he thought, that was an expression, considering the situation. He swallowed. "You can take it from here. The state buried my mother so you might want to know why and how she died...No, I'm not returning to Hawaii. I have nothing here. My life is elsewhere. Good-bye and good luck." He hung up and turning saw the towel draped figure.

"You did it. Why?"

Wayne walked to his wife and put his arms around her and rested his face on her wet head. "I've been thinking about it all week. I think you're right. He may be continuing with his need with other children and he has to be stopped. I didn't mention that problem but they will investigate him and hopefully there will be complaints against him. He may not be responsible for my mother's death. Tony said she suffocated over a period of a few days. That would be what...second degree murder? I don't know if he knew she could suffocate with the tape over her mouth and stuffed in that closet. Anyway, I put the ball in their park and we are leaving, hopefully to never be heard from again." He held her even closer and kissed her wet forehead.

"Thank you darling." Erin whispered into his chest. "I'm so proud of you."

"I wanted to show you how much I love you. I was so afraid it would destroy our lives. I was being selfish, to save us our privacy." She looked up at him. "You think that by now I don't know how much you love me? I know that I am cherished and loved. You make me feel it with everything you do. I'm sure the mystery won't be picked up in the mainland papers, certainly not in San Diego. It's an old killing and your father may have an alibi for that time. They many never get anything on him but I agree with you now. You don't have to be involved. Let the police worry about finding the facts. We will enjoy our last day here tomorrow and then fly home.

We haven't even discussed all of the work we have ahead of us after we get home. We have to get you moved out of your apartment and your furniture to the Salvation Army. Then we can get you settled into my place. We should have gotten some of that taken care of before we left."

"Don't worry about it, Babe. I had boxed up most of my personal things, anything I wanted to keep, so it really won't be that much of a job to move. In fact it's going to be fun moving in with you. This place has been a fun 'home' for this month and you have amazed me with the meals you have been able to do in this small kitchen." He motioned to the kitchenette there in the single room. "But the fun time will be living together in your apartment. We can really make that our home until we can save enough to buy our first house."

"I know. I'm looking forward to it too. In fact, I can hardly wait. I don't want to leave here. It's been so wonderful but I'm also looking forward to starting our lives in San Diego. It's going to be fun telling Doris all about this month, everything we've seen. I wonder if Paul has made any headway with her or if Joel is staying in touch. I guess with all of that ahead of us I'm beginning to get excited about going home. Who would think I would look forward to ending our honeymoon." She suddenly laughed. "I think I had better get some clothes on. Which, bathing suit or shorts?"

"I think we've beached it for today. Do you need any groceries for dinner tonight or should we fun shop? You haven't found a souvenir to take home to Doris have you? This might be the time to do that."

"I have the food for our dinner but my gosh, you're right, we haven't gotten a gift for Doris. What would you suggest? Do you think she would like one of the coral or shell necklaces?"

"Honey, you know her better than I do. Does she have clothes to go with the Hawaiian necklaces? How about something in wood?"

"Yes, that could work. Guess we'd better do some shopping. We wouldn't want to put it off until tomorrow. Do you want to take something home to Paul?"

Wayne thought about it a few minutes. "I don't think so...men don't usually do that kind of thing...do they?"

"Probably not, but he was very helpful with our wedding and toting everyone around for us. I just thought maybe we could find some little thing he might like as a thanks."

"Well...he's into fish. Maybe one of the carved fish we have seen would please him."

"That sounds good. I'll get dressed and then we can go see what we can find."

"Babe...would you like to have a special dinner out tomorrow night? The last night of our honeymoon?"

"How about our having a simple dinner here and then sitting on the beach to watch the sunset? We could take our beach towels, a bottle of champagne and glasses and we can stay there as long as we want to. We could do a little of our packing tomorrow afternoon before dinner so we wouldn't be pushed when we get back. We can have a relaxed bedtime and enjoy every minute of it."

"Oh, fella, I do like your ideas. We could have been sunset watching every night. Why didn't we think of it before? It will make a perfect last night. Let's do our shopping now...guess I'd better get clothes on first. Why do I keep putting that off?" She laughed. "I think I've found a new wonderful way of life."

Chapter 15

"Would you like a beverage?" She leaned closer to the tanned couple and said, "By any chance have you been on your honeymoon?"

Erin blushed as she looked up at the flight attendant. "I can't believe this…it's gotten to be funny. How did you know?"

"I've been a flight attendant with Delta for eleven years. You get to know your passengers. Honeymooners sort of stick out to us."

"We were married a month ago and have been honeymooning in Hawaii ever since." bragged Wayne.

"My, you were fortunate. What a wonderful honeymoon. You look as if you enjoyed it."

Erin smiled and nodded her head.

"Would you like a champagne? Curtesy of Delta."

"Oh, that would be fun. A nice way to end our hon…vacation. Thank you."

The attendant smiled at the couple and reached into the cart and brought out two bottles of champagne about the size of a small coke. 'Splits.' She would remember to give them a large bottle from the crew at the end of the flight. They could celebrate again when they got to their home. A policy of Delta Air was to make flights memorable for the passengers, especially when the flights were very special like weddings, anniversaries and big birthdays. A flight can add or spoil a special occasion and the airlines worked to make them happy. Their crews were trained to treat passengers as they would guests in their homes and it paid off. June Haley had recognized the young couple in 28A & B as recently married. They were obviously very much in love and her ring looked new. Not all newlyweds looked this much in love or at least it wasn't this obvious. She loved seeing it and knew she would go home to her husband tomorrow feeling more in love and grateful for his love. This was a good job, mostly because of the people you met and the crews you worked with but she did miss her husband when sleeping over in hotels. The novelty of sharing a room with some of the other stewardesses had gotten old very early. Now it was just a necessary part of the job. She would call Phil as soon as she was in her room. She was hungry to hear his voice.

    She continued to push her beverage cart down the aisle filling drink orders and passing out pretzels. Lunch and then the movie would help to fill the long flight for the passengers as well as the staff. She would give the newlyweds champagne as a gift from the crew but she'd also have them sign a card to go with it. A piece of paper she could draw hearts and an arrow on. It was always a challenge to find paper to use for cards. Delta should keep paper or even birthday and anniversary cards in with the supplies on board so the staff wouldn't have to use scratch paper. A napkin might have to do

    Erin and Wayne had raised the arm rest between them so they could sit closer and hold hands without too many people noticing. They were surprised when the attendant recognized them as honeymooners. Erin wondered again if it was obvious to everyone. Did their love for each other show that much? She looked at Wayne. He looked the same to her. She giggled. It must be her. Her happiness as a bride must give them away. How long would it show? The rest of her life she hoped. She could never love Wayne more than she did now. He had shared his past life with her…his pains and his few joys and she had loved him more as she offered her strength and a possible solution about his father. She felt so much closer to him. They were a real team, not just lovers. They had solved problems together and she knew it would always be that way. She smiled and settled down in her seat and watched out the small window at the beautiful blue sky and a sea of white clouds as Wayne held her hand while fingering her wedding ring.

The descent into Lindbergh airport was always a steep one. It was considered one of the most dangerous because of it's hills and tall buildings under the flight path. They watched the buildings pass beneath the plane and then waited for the landing. It was a good one. No jolts or bounces. Wayne continued to hold Erin's hand until they had pulled into the gate.

They sat in their seats until most of the other passengers had left and then slowly unbuckled their seatbelts. Their Hawaiian honeymoon was over. Wayne pulled their carry-ons down from the bulkhead and followed Erin down the aisle. The attendant greeted them and handed Erin a bottle wrapped in a Delta towel and a hand-drawn card with two large hearts with an arrow through it. with the message "Congratulations." Erin opened the folded paper. Inside it was signed by the entire staff.

"Thank you, oh thank you. This was a perfect ending for our trip" She looked at the smiling faces of the flight crew who were standing in the doorway of the cockpit. "Thank you, this is wonderful." The happy looks on the couples faces is all the crew needed. This was a marriage that would last.

Doris was the first person Erin saw. Behind her was Paul. Doris was jumping up and down in excitement, waving her arms so they wouldn't miss her.

Erin laughed. How would anyone possibly miss Doris. She had a feeling their return wasn't the only thing that was adding to her excitement. Paul was beaming as he waved to them.

Erin threw her arms around Doris and kissed her cheek.

"Oh my gosh are you ever tan. You look fantastic!" Doris gushed.

"Doris you wouldn't believe that air...and the warm salty water. It's wonderful! Hi. Paul... how are you?" She let go of Doris and moved over to him and gave him a big hug.

Wayne leaned down and gave Doris a kiss and then shook Paul's hand. "You guys are great to come pick us up. Would you believe we missed you?" Wayne laughed as he patted Paul on his shoulder. "We each have a bag at baggage claim and since we are about the last people off the plane the bags will probably be there by now.

"What held you up getting off? I was beginning to worry you had missed the plane. Not that I would have blamed you if you had just stayed on in Hawaii. It must have been really great."

"Doris, you wouldn't believe how wonderful those beaches are. The sand is so deep and white you can hardly walk on it. The water is so warm it's like a bath. We loved it."

"How was your honeymoon motel?" Doris asked.

Wayne and Erin looked at each other and then laughed.

Erin put her hand on her friends arm as they walked the long halls. "You wouldn't believe. Oh Doris, you wouldn't believe how terrible it was."

"Oh, no! Was it really? What did you do? What was wrong with it? Didn't you plan to stay there the whole month?"

Paul looked at Wayne. "What did you do?"

"You wouldn't believe how awful it was Paul. We can laugh about it now but, God, it was awful. It had a bedroom, bath, a living room and a little kitchen fully furnished but I wouldn't let Erin cook. Everything was so grimy. We left after a couple of days...told the owner we had an emergency family call so had to leave. He was very sympathetic and let us out of our lease, I guess you would call it. Anyway a waitress told us about a place in Waikiki. She knew someone, actually a sister I guess, who worked there and it gave us an 'in'. We had a one room apartment, fully furnished, five minutes from the beach and near shopping. We had a car so we were pretty free to go wherever we wanted to. We saw some of the tourist things but our favorites were the beaches as you can tell from our color. You'll have to go there someday soon. See, I was right, our bags are on the carousel, almost alone."

"When I saw you, I thought you were natives who lived in Hawaii. Paul teased. You really have a tan, buddy. I've never seen you pick up this much of a tan before. I've always thought we had a pretty good sun in San Diego. Maybe you'd like to move to Hawaii so you can look this healthy all the time." He stopped talking when he saw his friends face. The smile was gone and a cloud seemed to cover his eyes.

Paul was a little surprised with Wayne's reaction. He wondered what could have happened during the honeymoon that would have made him so uptight over such a simple suggestion. Well, if it was important, Paul was sure Wayne would eventually tell him.

"I was lucky to get a parking space my second time around. It's right over there. How was that for luck?"

"Pretty good, I'd say." Wayne had turned serious but polite. The girls followed, busy with their talk. Wayne was sure Doris would have heard all about their month before they even got to the car but he knew Erin would keep his life's secret. She wouldn't share it even with Doris. It was something he had to share with his wife but it would be just between them. The crack from Paul about his looking like a native of Hawaii; Wayne knew the remark was innocent, just a compliment about his tan, but it hit too close to his secret and his pain. Paul could never know how deep he had hit.

Watching Erin and Doris enjoying their reunion, he suddenly wondered that if he hadn't seen his old friend, would he have felt it necessary to tell Erin? Probably not, but he realized the knot in his middle was gone. Sharing with Erin, finally letting go of his life with his parents had been a release and it felt good. He wouldn't allow himself to think of Aunt Mary. She and his mother were buried where they belonged. Their deaths had been accidents so he wasn't really a murderer. Certainly not in God's eyes, so he wouldn't think about them anymore. His life with Erin was his future. The past was behind him.

The drive to La Jolla took about twenty minutes and Erin's apartment looked good. They were finally home. Home to their new life together. When Wayne had his things here they would really be starting their life. They were playing house in Hawaii. This would be real.

Erin opened her apartment door and put her overnight bag down just inside. Doris followed into the apartment that until recently had also been her home. Paul carried in Erin's bag and Wayne followed with his large bag.

"Do these go into the bedroom, Erin?"

"Yes, thanks. Put them on the bed and we can unpack from there. I've left lots of hangers for your things, Wayne." She walked into the bedroom and opened the closet door. "Oh my gosh, oh my gosh. Your clothes are here. Darling look, your things are here." She turned around to look at Doris. "You did this?"

"Paul and I did. In fact, Wayne, you are all moved out of your apartment. We felt there wasn't any reason for you to pay another month's rent just for your things. Sooooooe we moved your boxes and clothes here and took the furniture you had said you were going to give to the Salvation Army. They were pleased to get all of it. Hope you don't mind but we did hang your clothes and put some in the drawers Erin had emptied. Some things you will have to find places for. We hope it helped."

"Helped. I would say it helped. We had expected to spend the rest of the weekend doing all of that." Wayne looked at their friends. "You are truly the best. How can we ever thank you?"

Doris smiled. "You can thank us by letting us take you both out to dinner tonight to celebrate your homecoming. We have missed you both. I tried to put food in the refrigerator but I know Erin will need to get a little settled back in and organized before she can plan a dinner around the food I bought. Soooo, we are taking you out."

"No way! You have done all of this for us and you will be our guests. I insist on that!"

"Wayne, now you are embarrassing us. We wouldn't have suggested dinner if we thought you were going to pay. You have been buying some meals out on your month's honeymoon. This is on us…or Paul and I are leaving and you can fend for yourselves. Come to think of it…maybe that is what you would prefer." Doris laughed.

"You two. I can't believe this. Well…we will just have to catch up with you another time and I for one will gladly accept your dinner invitation. You just don't realize how much you helped. Wayne is having to go to San Francisco on Monday and now we will be able to relax a little after our flight and all. Do we need to go back to the apartment to vacuum and scrub a little?"

"Nope, it's all done. You're out and I also have your deposit check for you but you are not going to use it for this dinner."

Erin and Wayne gave their friends hugs. They had run out of words. Loving friendships are so rare. Friends like this… they were truly blessed.

"Well, I guess we lost that argument but I think we'll want to change clothes before we go. We have been in these all day. Also, we have some little things we found for you in Hawaii. Will we be late if we change and get the packages out of the suitcase?"

"I don't think so Erin…we took this into consideration when we made the reservations." She smiled. "At least the changing clothes part…but packages…that sounds exciting. I think we can find time for both." Doris laughed. "Erin knows how much I like packages. We have time and I promise you we have chosen a casual restaurant so you don't need to dress up. We're going to the Bajia Lobster. Does that sound all right?"

"It not only sounds all right it's wonderful…one of our favorites."

"Well, we promise we won't keep you out late. You've had a long day but I think we need to get going soon so change if you want to and then bring out the packages. We can wait." Doris grinned. "I don't know what you brought for us but we will give you time to get them. I do like gifts."

"Erin laughed…how good it was to be back with close friends. "Okay, we'll hurry. A quick wash up is all I need but I will change my blouse and jacket. How about you Wayne?"

"I could use a shower but won't take the time now if you have reservations. I will change my shirt. Cum mon bride. Let's get to it. Turn on the TV if you want to, Paul. You can relax while we're changing. How much time do we have?"

"Half an hour…at least." Paul said.

"We can make that. I have found that Erin is a quick change artist when she wants to be and I can even shower and dress in that length of time. I think that will just give us package time too." He said laughing. This is what life was all about…real life. Life with good friends and the person you loved. Wayne felt himself relax and it was good."

Wayne followed Erin into their bedroom and closed the door as Paul turned on the television and Doris picked up a magazine from the coffee table and started thumbing through it. No sense in getting into a TV show and then having to leave in the middle.

She looked up at Paul. and grinned.

"I think we did it Paul. They seemed really pleased and relieved they don't have that moving job ahead of them. You had a wonderful idea and I loved helping you. Thanks for including me, but remember, I'm sharing with the dinner cost tonight. This is something WE are doing together for them. Not just you, okay?" She laughed. "That means do you understand what I have said… not is it alright!"

Paul smiled. "Okay." He said.

Erin was first out of the bedroom and had changed into a matching light beige knit slacks, tee shirt, jacket and bone sandals. Her hair was brushed down around her shoulders and face. She was back in San Diego clothes but with a Hawaii tan.

"If it won't be too much of a strain on you why don't we save the packages until after dinner." She looked at Doris and Paul for confirmation. Paul nodded his head in agreement but Doris, being Doris gave her a big pout and then a smile. "Okay then. I'd like to also suggest that I ride in the back of the car with Doris and you men can chauffeur us. Doris and I haven't had much 'talking' time and I know you guys always have things to talk about. Men talk."

"I second that vote, Erin. I've really missed you. I don't think we have been apart for a month since we have known each other. I do have lots of 'woman' talk I can hardly wait to share with you."

The bedroom door opened and Wayne came out looking fresh. His hair was still a little wet so he had obviously taken time for his shower. He'd changed into 'suntans' with a navy cotton shirt. His dark tan almost matched his brown hair. Hawaii had obviously been good for both of them.

"Wayne, we just voted that the 'girls' would sit together in the back seat and you and I can 'catch up' in the front.

Wayne glanced at Erin with a little concern but then relaxed. He didn't have to worry about her. "Okay, I guess I can give you up for a few minutes." He winked at Erin then turned to Paul. "What shall we talk about, Paul?" He looked at his friend with a broad grin and Paul felt their friendship was tight again.

The drive was short but Erin was able to ask the questions uppermost in her mind. She quietly whispered to Doris so as to not be heard by the men. "You and Paul seem pretty close. Has more developed with you while we were gone? What happened to your crush with Joel?"

Doris put her hand on Erin's arm and leaned close to her. "Paul and I are friends. He has been very attentive and helpful, especially with moving Wayne but Erin, Joel calls every other day. I am so happy I can hardly stand it. He sounds serious. In fact he wants to send me money for a plane ticket to San Francisco. He wants me to see 'his' town."

"Oh, my gosh, that does sound serious. Are you ready for this kind of a relationship? I guess that was a dumb question. You have always had a crush on Joel but now it sounds like more. This is so exciting. Doris, you would be my sister in law. I'm so excited…can I tell Wayne?"

"Sure but don't blow it up too much yet. Things might not work out but. oh Erin.

I've never been happier. I am so much in love."

Erin leaned over as far as her seat belt would allow and gave her best friend a big hug. I feel a little sorry for Paul. Does he know what has developed between you and Joel?"

"I have laid hints and I have kept my distance from him. I mention what a good 'friend' he is. I hate to hurt his feelings and you never know, this thing with Joel may not work out. It has been mostly a phone romance. We have to be together in person more to see if it's real. That's one reason I accepted the San Francisco trip."

"My gosh! When are you going?"

"We are talking in a couple of weeks."

"Too bad you can't leave Monday. Wayne is driving to San Francisco and it could save you, or Joel one plane ticket. How long will you stay?"

"Just for a weekend. I can't take time off right now. It will be a good start for us. We can find out lots in a weekend but thanks for the suggestion. Would you really have trusted me with Wayne for that drive?" She laughed as Erin poked her in the side.

"Doris, I'd trust Wayne with my life. He is the most moral person I have ever known and I adore him."

"Erin, I'm so happy for you. I just hope Joel and I can find what you two have."

Chapter 16

It's a nine hour drive from San Diego to San Francisco but Wayne took three days to see his customers in all of the towns between.

Each night he called Erin. She too was again entrenched in her job and back into familiar routines except she admitted it all felt different. She was married now and was still finding things to do in the apartment to make it more theirs instead of Doris and hers. She missed his being next to her at night. He ached terribly from wanting her and was determined to make it home by the weekend even if it meant driving all night. They both needed the weekend to be together again.

This would often be their schedules as long as Wayne had the sales job but Erin's dream for him was his own parts store. If they both worked hard and saved as much as possible they could possibly get a loan. With only one rent to pay now seven hundred dollars could be put away each month toward their dream. It would build fast and in two to three years they could have their own business.

Neither one of them had family to turn to for help. Certainly, Wayne didn't and she wouldn't ask the boys because they were just building their lives. Aunt Mary...she would never ask her for money. How could she when her aunt had been so against the marriage she hadn't even attended and this had hurt her deeply. Aunt Mary...she hadn't heard anything from her and she didn't feel like making the first call...at least not yet! She was blunt and outspoken at times. Her words could hurt but most of the time she was loving and even generous to her. The 'boys' had never paid much attention to relatives and Aunt Mary had only tolerated them when they were around but had stepped in for her after their parents had died. She was an adviser, a friend, and she missed her.

Erin knew she would have to swallow her pride and would go to the house before Wayne returned. She would see her aunt alone for a while and was sure that eventually Wayne would be accepted. Who could not love a man who had so much love and caring to give?

For Wednesday and Thursday nights in San Francisco, Wayne had chosen a Budget Inn. He had a room with a desk for his evening paper work, a television for a little relaxing and complimentary breakfasts that were brought to his room in the early mornings. A pot of coffee, Creamora and sugar packages, a fresh different sweet roll each morning and a small glass of canned orange juice. A home away from home... missing only Erin. A heated pool always beckoned him after a full sales and traveling day. Now he planned to take his dip before calling Erin so her voice would be the last one he heard before going to sleep.

The two calls he'd had after returning to San Diego still bothered him. He wasn't really worried but knowing the case of his mother's death had been reopened and the detectives in Hawaii wanting to interview him personally. They had found him...what else would they find?...well, let them find his father first...let him prove he didn't do it...let them prove he had put his mother in the closet...as she had done to him so many times. Let them prove he was responsible when he was already in San Diego. Delta records could prove that. He hadn't put his mother in the closet to die, it wasn't planned. He had known it was the only way he could escape her but he had no remorse over the outcome. He had never felt a moment of love from her or a moment of feeling wanted. He was a disappointment to her and to his father, only because the sexual gratification would have been sweeter for his father.

Well he had suffered the pain and humiliation for those years but was grateful it was him and not an innocent little girl. The thought of a sweet little girl, as Erin had once been being so abused about tore him up. He would protect Erin and any child they had with his life…if necessary.

His second day in San Francisco had been successful. His customers were glad to see him and anxious to learn about their month in Hawaii. A month in Hawaii at any time…often an experience lived through others. The Hawaii tan hadn't faded yet and it wasn't the norm in San Francisco so Wayne felt a little self conscious. It had been many years since he'd had this color year round, in spite of the hours he was forced to stay inside. Now it was a treat and he was proud of the honeymoon he and Erin had accomplished. Meeting up with his old friend hadn't been expected or planned. Finding that his father was back in town was a shock but they had been able to handle it. Being open and truthful, except for the closet, with Erin had felt wonderful and he had vowed he would always be truthful with her. They would have a good marriage. A marriage built on trust.

Wayne had felt relaxed with his customers and the orders had built up…larger than usual. They would build his commission and if the rest of this week or the rest of this month was as successful it would help toward building their dream; Erin's dream that had seemed impossible to him but was now their dream. It was a dream that would become a reality and sooner than they had expected.

Wayne grabbed a bacon burger and chocolate shake at the Wendy's a block from the hotel. He was hungry for food but more hungry for Erin's voice. Tonight he would call her first then take his swim. He could relive their conversation when swimming his laps. It was wonderful to be loved and to love...he had missed so much.

The phone rang four times before Erin answered.

"Hi, what are you up to?"

"Hi, yourself. I've been waiting for your call but you caught me in my shower. My hair is dripping and I'm wrapped in a towel...but I guess you don't mind."

"You're driving me crazy. I remember how you look after your shower. Just wish I was there with you. How was your day?"

"Fine except for missing you. I can keep busy during the day but dinner time and the nights are lonely. I never realized before how lonely they could be. I called Aunt Mary several times... even from the office but she hasn't answered. I can't believe she left town for this whole month without telling me before the wedding."

"Darling, hadn't she talked of taking an European trip recently? Do you suppose she chose this time to do it?"

"But wouldn't she have told me?"

"Maybe an opening came up suddenly. I'm sure you'll be getting a postcard soon from some far off place. I wouldn't worry about her. She's just being independent."

"I have driven past the house several times and the garden is looking terrible. I don't think her gardener has done a thing. I know where she keeps her trimmers in the garage so I think I'll go over and cut back a few things. If she isn't home by this weekend maybe you'll cut the grass. She couldn't help but love you for that." Erin laughed.

"Wayne, I miss you so much. I guess it's going to take me a while to get used to your being gone after the fabulous month we had."

"It was pretty fabulous, wasn't it! I'll be home early

Saturday morning. I'm planning on driving Friday night so we can have the weekend together."

"That idea scares me, Wayne. Honey, you will have been driving all around San Francisco and it's outskirts, getting orders all day. Then, for you to drive nine hours more to get home...I don't want anything to happen to you, darling. I want you home too but..."

"I promise I'll stop for a nap if I get sleepy. I want to be home safely too. I'll be careful, I promise. Well, you'd better get some dry clothes on and dry that dripping hair. You probably have a puddle to mop up now. I'll call tomorrow night. I love you, Erin. Take care of yourself...talk to you tomorrow."

"Yes, all right darling. I'll hug your pillow all night. Hope you have a good day tomorrow. Goodnight sweetheart...goodbye...Wayne!...I love you. Goodnight."

"I love you too. Goodnight."

Wayne slowly hung up the receiver, hating to lose the sound of her voice.

He suddenly felt drained and lonely. He would pass on the swim tonight. Instead he pulled the spread back from one side of the king sized bed and then pulled back the blanket and top sheet, lowered himself onto the mattress and pulled the covers up to his neck. The pillow was soft so he snuggled his shoulder into it and in minutes was asleep.

Thursday was another successful day and Wayne wondered if his new happy attitude reflected on his customers. It had always been just a job before but now he felt inspired to promote as much merchandise as he could. To be sure his customers were well informed about new products and to be sure they would have enough parts to last until his next visit in a month.

Lunch had been sparse as he had more distance between

customers to travel that day and then back to his base hotel.

He had felt a gnawing discomfort about Erin's plans to work on the shrubbery at her Aunt Mary's that evening so when he got back to his room he called her before he went for his dinner or swim. He let the phone ring eight times before he hung up. Seven thirty...she could still be at the house so he made a quick run back to Wendy's for another hamburger and shake. Erin wouldn't have approved but he needed what he considered. 'comfort food.'

When he returned to his room he could hear his phone ringing and he fumbled with the card key trying to get the damn door open before she hung up.

"Hi!"

"Hi, you sound out of breath. Did I get you out of the shower this time?"

"No. I called you at seven thirty but decided you were still trimming bushes at Aunt Mary's so I ran out for a hamburger. I heard the phone ringing when I got back to the room but couldn't get the card to open the door. I was sure it was you and I was afraid you'd hang up."

"No. I had such an exciting experience when trimming the bougainvillea I couldn't wait for your call to tell you."

"Was your aunt home?" Wayne almost choked on his words.

"No and I didn't go in the house but I will tomorrow but honey, let me tell you what I found."

Wayne took a deep breath trying to not let Erin hear it. He tried to sound interested. "What could you find gardening that would make you so excited?"

"A window, Wayne. I found a window."

Wayne pulled the receiver away from his face and put his forehead in his left hand for a minute.

"Wayne, are you there?"

He put the receiver back to his ear. "A window....you were trimming and found a window? Where was it? Buried under bushes?"

"No darling...on the wall behind the bougainvillea. It had completely covered it."

"What was behind the window?" Wayne asked, trying to sound casual.

"I don't know, I couldn't tell. There is a shade pulled down shutting out the room. I'll go into the house tomorrow. I should check it out anyway. Maybe I'll find a note for me or a clue as to where Aunt Mary has gone."

Wayne felt a stab in his middle. It was over. Erin would find the wall. She would go to the room and feel it needed more light and even a view of the vine. She would know the window had to be there, somewhere...she would find Aunt Mary's body. Oh, God! he couldn't protect her from that. He couldn't protect their marriage...It had been so short. Erin. She would suffer...he couldn't protect her from that either.

It might take a little time for him to be suspected of killing her but then who else would have a reason? No, they'd know. Maybe, as hard as it would be to accept, Erin would know he had done it. How could he ever face her again? How could he see that pain and maybe even hate on her precious face? Her little pixie look filled his mind. He could never see her again. He could save her that. He could save her his trial, his imprisonment. She would want to be loyal; he couldn't handle that.

"Darling...you are so quiet. Did I catch you at a bad time? Did you have a bad day? Honey, are you all right?"

"No, sweetheart, you didn't catch me at a bad time. Actually I'm having a very good week and I'm feeling fine. A few more of these weeks and I'll have replaced the amount we had saved and spent on our honeymoon. We'll be that much ahead. I'm finding that being so much in love and married has given even my job a new outlook. I think we'll have our shop sooner than we thought." Wayne took three quiet breaths.

"I'm just a little concerned about your going into your aunt's home alone. How about waiting until Saturday when I can go with you?"

"Oh, Wayne, would you really mind if I do it tomorrow? I'm so excited about it. It's kind of fun. I really feel like a detective and I can hardly wait to check it out. You and I will have so much to do Saturday but first you'll need some sleep after your long drive. I need to take care of you. I want so much to be a good wife." She took a quick breath. "In fact, I'm going to set the alarm so I can be up waiting for you when you get home."

A pain grabbed Wayne's chest and he felt sick to his stomach.

"How about being wakened by a kiss from your prince. Wouldn't that be better? I'd hate to have you sitting, waiting, and I can kiss you awake and then crawl in next to you so I can hold you in my arms for the rest of the night. Then, after breakfast, we can go to Aunt Mary's."

"My prince huh? That does sound good. Mmmmm, I'll be waiting for that kiss but I still think I'll try to find that hidden window. Tomorrow night you'll be home and I'm looking forward to being in your arms again too. I can hardly wait. It's been a long week and I've missed you so much. I'll never get used to these weeks without you."

"I know, sweetheart but for the first time in my life I have something to work for and someone to come home to. You'll never, never know how much that has meant, does mean to me. Your love has made my life. I don't know how I've been so lucky. I thank God for you everyday. You gave me faith in him, you know, and faith that he will forgive my sins. I now believe we have spirits and souls we can share with others. You, my precious wife, will always have my spirit with you, even when I'm away."

"I know, Wayne. I have felt you with me every day. I guess love like ours does that. Have you really felt me with you?"

"All the time." He tried to laugh. "Especially when I got you out of the shower...a delightful image. I could hardly sleep that night."

Erin laughed and Wayne felt he had never heard anything so beautiful.

"Wayne, you won't really mind if I go into Aunt Mary's tomorrow, will you?

I'll wait if you insist but I'd really rather go then...I'm so excited about solving the mystery of the window...I thought I knew that house pretty well but something seems different."

"Erin," Wayne said in a serious tone. "Go if you really want to but do one thing for me."

"Of course, always, what is it?"

"I don't want you going in there alone...that house has been empty for over a month...you just don't know what you'll find. Please call Paul and ask him to go with you. That's all I'll ask."

Erin was quiet for a minute. Wayne wondered what was going through her mind. He was realizing that either day she went she would be in for a big shock. It could be better to have Paul with her. If he was with her could he keep her from discovering 'the wall'? He doubted it. He could visualize her checking where the red bougainvillea was and then comparing the room to it's location. She would knock on the wall...listening for it's supports and when hearing the hollow sound and maybe seeing the wall give a little, would investigate further. It was the kind of woman she was, this love of his.

"Honey, I'll call Paul tonight. I'm sure he will feel the way you do. Maybe I'll have a fun mystery all solved. Darling. I have thought that there might be a note from Aunt Mary. I should have gone in before this but I was hurt; so sure she was staying away to hurt me because I wouldn't listen to her when she talked against you."

"Erin. Maybe you should have listened to your aunt."

"Wayne, how can you say that? Darling, are you worried about becoming involved with your mother's murder? You can prove you were in San Diego when she died. Your father must have killed her, just as you said, and now he feels safe. If your old friend hadn't been on that beach, you wouldn't have known he was still alive and certainly you wouldn't have known he was in Pearl City. You didn't have to call the police and tell them what you suspected. You wouldn't do that if you were guilty.

You are the most loving, kind, gentle man I have ever known. You wouldn't have killed your mother even after everything she did to you. Your father, he was sick and brutal. Of course he killed her and they'll prove it!"

Wayne listened to her with tears in his eyes. He didn't deserve her trust, her love…and now he had killed it all. "Erin, you are my heart…I love you so much."

"I love you too, Wayne. I can hardly wait for you to be home. Hurry home, darling, you are my prince."

"Erin, don't put me on a pedestal. It's too hard to stay there. I'd hate to have you disappointed. I don't want to hurt you…if I do, it's because it was beyond my control."

"Wayne, I might disappoint you someday. Guess all we can do is try our best and always love each other."

"That will always be…you will always be my love, my life."

His tears began to flow.

"Erin, I have paper work to clear up before tomorrow...we'd better end this. Just remember how much I love you. Have a good night's sleep and let Paul help you tomorrow and whenever I'm not there." Wayne wiped his face and took a deep breath and tried to control his voice. "He's a good friend. You can count on him. Wish I were there to kiss you goodnight but I'll dream about your kisses and holding you."

"I'll dream about you too but it's only one more night honey; just one more night until you'll waken me with your kiss. Remember?" She laughed.

"Yes, just one more night. How could I forget? Sleep well my love." Then softly, "Goodbye."

"Goodnight, darling ...I love you." She wasn't sure he had heard her. He had hung up.

Wayne fell onto his knees next to the bed and sobbed until he was exhausted.

He had to call 'the boys.' They wouldn't understand his being in San Francisco and not calling them.

Sitting on the floor, his back against the bed, Wayne reached for the phone and realized he had gotten only half of the receiver on the cradle. He straightened it and then pulled his address book from the desk and looked up Joel and Jerry's number. Brothers living together. God, he had missed so much. He wiped his swollen eyes, blew his nose and just sat against the bed until he could talk... then dialed.

"Joel...this is Wayne. Yeah. I'm in San Fran...been here since Wednesday but I've been traveling around seeing my customers so haven't had time to call before this. I'm leaving tomorrow night; thought I'd drive straight through. I've a wife to get home to." He laughed but the laugh had no humor. "I thought maybe we could meet for lunch if your schedules are free or even a quick dinner before I leave. Yeah. I'm at the Budget Inn at San Mateo. Dinner? Sounds good if we can make it early. Five is good. Yeah, we had a great month. Hawaii is the best. I'll bore you with the details when I see you. I just talked with Erin...she's great...just worried about her aunt. She's going to the house tomorrow after work. No, she hasn't heard from Aunt Mary but she's done some pruning and watering. Seems the gardener hasn't been there recently. You know if you're not there to be on top of them they just don't show. Seems to be the norm for gardeners and contractors these days." He took a couple of deep breaths while holding the phone from his mouth. 'Well, I have to hit the paper work...orders have been good this week. Hope it keeps up. Yeah, I'll see you at 5:00. Okay, okay, sounds good. Oh, Joel, we sure appreciated your coming down for the wedding. You made Erin really happy. Okay, see you....bye." He hung up.

Wayne knew he had used the paper work as an excuse to end both conversations. He now wished he'd talked to Joel before he called Erin---he wished Erin's voice was the last he heard. He could call her again but was afraid it would worry her. They'd had a long conversation ...longer than usual. What had he said? 'Remember, he had always loved her' then 'Bye' That could have been a big slip. Hopefully she wouldn't catch it. Until later...

The daily report didn't take long and he neatly placed it with the orders. He addressed an envelope, placed the orders and the log in the envelope, sealed and stamped it and put it back on the desk for mailing tomorrow.

The dinner had been a mistake. He used the bathroom and then pulled on his swim trunks and a tee shirt for the walk to the pool.

He slipped his feet into thongs and then, as a second thought, took a pair of clean sun-tans and a navy, long sleeved shirt from the suitcase and hung them on hangers 'for tomorrow'.

He looked around the room. Everything was in order. Clothes out, his shaver and such on the sink. He threw the tee shirt he usually slept in casually on the bed then took a magazine that had been left in the room---ironically a magazine featuring Hawaii as a wonderful vacation get away---opened it to the Hawaiian article and placed it open on the bed next to his tee shirt. It would look as if he meant to read it.

The hallway was empty and he headed outside to the pool. He had it to himself so pulled off his shirt, spread the bath towel he had taken from the bathroom on a padded recliner. The sun was gone now but it was a good time for a long, refreshing swim.

Wayne looked around him at the motel, the parked cars and then the headlights on the freeway. People going home to their families…their loved ones. Tears came to his eyes.

He slowly eased himself into the cool water and reclined his body down until he was totally wet and then began swimming toward the deep end of the pool. There he did what he considered a racing turn and headed back to the shallow end.

At first his mind was racing. What had he forgotten? Would his body soil the pool? He would hate to be responsible for the cost of having it drained and cleaned.

Erin. What would she find tomorrow? Would she know? Would she then suspect about his mother? Poor, darling Erin. She didn't deserve this. They had hoped for so much more. So many, many years together. His arms were getting tired as he pulled them through the water. Eight laps…more…so many more to go. His legs were tired of kicking but he kept going back and forth, back and forth. In spite of being raised in Hawaii he wasn't a strong swimmer… going swimming only when he was able to sneak away from the house. He had taught himself to get through the water. It meant punishment from his mother but he had loved the sandy beaches and the waves. Now he felt mechanical like a toy whose batteries were running down. That was him …his batteries were running down.

One more stroke…one more kick…again… again.

They say drowning was painless. Easy. Stroke, kick, they became slower as Wayne gradually stopped. His mind saw Erin's smiling face and he smiled back as the air bubbled from his lungs and his exhausted body settled to the bottom of the pool.

His feet hit the rough surface and instinctively pushed up. Coughing and splashing Wayne gasped for air and reached out for the edge of the pool. His fingers grabbed the tile and clung. He pulled his body to the rough side and tried to slowly control his breathing. Small breaths at first and then larger ones. The air felt good in his lungs and he looked up at the sky. Stars seemed to look back. He put his head down on his hands and sobbed. His salty tears running into the pool. He hadn't been able to do it. The will to live was stronger. He knew he would have to face punishment for what he had done. He would have to face Erin, her brothers and their friends; his employers. He had tried so hard to leave his past behind him. He had tried to build a life and he had succeeded. Aunt Mary…if it hadn't been for Aunt Mary…she had won after all. He could hear her laughing from where ever she was. His father, his mother and Aunt Mary, they had known he wasn't any good and they had been right. How could he face Joel and Jerry tomorrow? He just wouldn't show for the dinner but would leave for San Diego in the morning. They would understand in a few days. The tears came harder and he choked on them.

Erin…his precious Erin.

A WALL WITHIN

Wayne moved slowly along the side of the pool to the metal ladder and grabbing hold of the bar closest to him, placed his left foot on the bottom rung then moved his right foot up to the second rung. His body felt like jelly so he rested a moment. He leaned over the top rung, spilling water onto the surface of the pool's edge. He forced himself to take deeper breaths. Slow but deep. He looked up at the sky again and started moving up, then off the ladder. As he stepped onto the tile around the edge of the pool his right foot slipped in the water from his body and his feet went out from under him and his body bent back toward the pool, his head hitting the rail. The crack of his head on the metal was the only sound followed by a soft swish as his body slid back into the pool and once again settled to the bottom. A pool of red wrapped his head and then slowly moved as a fine ribbon to the surface.

Chapter 17

Erin opened the screen door and stared at it. The screening was bowed out toward her. What kind of accident could Aunt Mary have had to cause this? Somebody must have fallen against it. Slowly she put the key in the lock, turned the key and opened the kitchen door. The house smelled foul...almost gagging her...so she left the door open and went into the living room and opened the front door for cross ventilation. The sun wouldn't set for over an hour so she didn't bother turning lights on. The ironing board was standing in front of the sink. Her wedding slip was draped over the board. Tears came to her eyes. Aunt Mary must have planned on attending the wedding...what happened? Where was she?

She heard some talking in the bedroom and hesitated until she realized it was the bedroom television. She slowly walked into the room and found the lamp next to the bed was on. Aunt Mary wouldn't have gone far and left the television and a lamp on and she wouldn't have left her bed unmade. It wasn't her way. The smell filled the house so she opened the bedroom window then walked back into the kitchen and opened the window above the sink, then looked in the refrigerator. It was stocked with fruit, vegetables and unfortunately, meat. It must have been here a while as it was getting very strong and she quickly closed the meat drawer.

Erin slowly walked through the house looking for a note, a letter, something from her to explain the absence; a travel folder... something...there was nothing. Nothing.

Back into the kitchen. The pantry door was open and a new unpainted shelf had been installed near the floor. Hadn't Wayne said something about Aunt Mary wanting a shelf built?

He had done it; but when? It had to have been just before the wedding. They had hoped it would let Aunt Mary get to know Wayne better…to be able to accept him and their marriage. Had Wayne mentioned building the shelf? She couldn't remember.

    The covered window didn't seem quite so important anymore. She wandered through the one story house again. A slip of paper lay on the floor just under the kitchen cabinet. A receipt for the shelving materials dated a week before their wedding. Erin was beginning to get really worried. The ironing board, the iron and her slip. She had to have been here at least the day before if not the day of the wedding. Something had made her leave quickly. She never would have left a television and a lamp on or a refrigerator full of food. The damaged screen door. What would have done that? She looked in her aunt's bedroom and then the bath again. Nothing. The guestroom. A small room she had stayed in a few times. Living so close there had been few reasons for her to stay over night. After her mother died she stayed one night for comfort. Comfort for each of them. The room looked so small now and so dark and it smelled terrible. Not musty as it would from being closed up for a long period. She couldn't identify the smell unless a dead rat or bird was in the room someplace. She pulled the short drape on the lone window aside, unlocked the window and pushed it up until it was fully open. The fresh air from the ocean quickly helped to cut down on the strong smell so she stood breathing it in for a few moments then ran outside and around the house. The bougainvillea was on a trellis outside a window. She slowly walked that side of the house. Aunt Mary's bathroom, her bedroom window, then the guest bedroom's opened window. She turned the corner, the bougainvillea, the second window. The guestroom shade. There was once a second window in the guestroom. Why was it covered over? She ran back into the house to the little room. A chest stood against what had to be the outside wall. She began tapping on the paneling. Her father could do anything with a hammer and saw and had taught her all he knew. She had been his right hand helper on all of the house projects. Now she listened to the wall. It sounded hollow except right in the middle. The window could be there. Excitedly she ran to the small tool drawer in the kitchen and took a hammer from it and then hurried back to the bedroom. She got down on her knees and put the claw of the hammer against the back of the baseboard and slowly pried it loose the length of the wall. According to her teaching she pulled each nail from the board and put them in a pile out of the way. Then she started on the right hand corner of the wall to work it loose. Some of the panel broke but if Aunt Mary really felt the new wall was necessary they could replace it. Then Erin pulled the splintered pieces that ran from the ceiling to the floor loose and laid them along a good wall. So far the job was neat and she would have little to clean up after uncovering the window.

The smell got stronger and she was sure she would find at least one dead critter. There would have to be an opening in the outside wall or foundation that would need patching; possibly behind the vine.

The room was beginning to darken as the sun went down so she turned on the wall switch. A single ceiling light went on. Getting down on her hands and knees again she started pulling at the wood to the left of the opened area. Something silver caught her attention. She reached into the hole and realized the wall was about a foot out from the old wall. Her hand touched something metal and she jumped, bringing her hand out quickly. That was silly as something metal wouldn't hurt her. Now…soft and furry… that would have been different. Again she reached for the item and put her hand around the cold surface and brought it out.

"It's Wayne's," a voice said behind her.

Erin jumped from fright. She hadn't heard Paul enter the house but then she had left both doors wide open. Anyone could have come in. She was grateful it was Paul.

How could it be Wayne's? She looked at the metal measuring tape. How would it have been left here unless Wayne had left it when working on the wall? He had built a kitchen pantry shelf but she hadn't heard anything about a wall.

"Lord, you gave me a start. I'd forgotten you were coming. Wayne didn't want me here alone and I have both doors wide open. That was dumb so I'm glad it was you. Well, now that you are here do you want to help me take down the rest of this wall? I think there is a dead animal behind it."

"I'd be glad to help. From the smell there are dead critters someplace. It is sure foul in here but are you sure your aunt won't mind?"

"If she does, we can just replace it, but this room needs light more than it does a wall for the chest of drawers. It also needs another open window. Ooops. Guess we had better take down those two pictures or she would be mad."

Paul walked to the remaining part of the wall and lifted the two framed prints from their single nails. "These wouldn't have withstood much of an earthquake. They'd have flown across the room at the slightest tremor. Here, let me have that hammer. I'll take the rest of this wall down."

Erin sat on her heels with the measuring tape in her hand and watched as Paul attacked the remaining four-by-eight panel. She had strange emotions as she watched him. They were tearing down a wall Wayne must have built and hadn't mentioned to her. They had been so busy just before the wedding, especially as Wayne was gone the week before. Would he have built it before he went on that last trip out of town before the wedding? Now Paul had taken over 'her' job. A job she had relished doing. She had looked forward to taking down that wall. After all, she was the one who had found it. It was her wall to take down. It wasn't fair.

Paul pulled off the remaining top half of the panel but the lower edge gave resistance. He pulled and pried at the nails that held to, what seemed to be, a one by three that went all across that end of the room, about a foot in from the outside wall. Bits of a short drape were pulling out with the panel. He put his hand with the hammer in behind the stuck panel so he could pound it from the back but something soft was in his way. Paul stood and looked at Erin. Quietly he said. "Does your aunt have a flashlight? I need a flashlight."

Erin stood and again walked back to the kitchen drawer and took out a powerful looking flashlight. She tested the beam and decided it would show Paul whatever he had to see behind the wall. He took the flashlight and turned it on as Erin sat back on her heels again, still holding the measuring tape.

Paul aimed the light behind the wall then pulled his arm back, dropped the flashlight to the floor and frantically started pulling at the paneling. The piece came off suddenly, throwing him off balance and then he stood looking at what seemed to be the lower half of a long plastic bag. The upper half still behind the left side of the wall. A terrible odor came from the opened enclosure. He looked at Erin. Her hand was covering her nose and mouth and her face was very pale…her eyes enormous as she stared at the black package. The cold silver measuring tape dropped from her hand. She couldn't breath…she couldn't move. She choked on the bile that rose to her throat She felt as if she were drowning.

"No…**Oh, No! My God! Oh** my poor darling **Wayne**…**What have you done?**"

Printed in the United States
65549LVS00002B/160-183